Marta Bleaches Everything
Book Two of the Housekeeping Detective Series

Cyndia Rios-Myers

This book is dedicated to Marta Del Rio Morales – the world's best grandmother. Thank you for loving me so fiercely. Thank you for loving my brother, sisters, and my cousins in a way that convinced us that we were your favorite grandchildren. I miss you so much. I'll *never* stop missing you.

Acknowledgments

The fire behind "Marta Two" is owed to Marta's fans. Paramount in my gratitude are Raquel Rios, Rebecca Johnson, and Kristi Devenyi - thank you for your keen eyes and your knowledge of all things Marta. Big thanks also go to my mom Cristina, my niece Ilani, my aunt Sara, my mother-in-law Shelley, my friends Jessica Fitzgerald, Tracy Born, Jennifer Miller, Christine Severy, Melissa Badour, Jasmin Culbertson, Jenny Black...and so many others!

My gratitude STILL goes to Perry Myers (no relation) of MSI Detective Services. My friends in maintenance services still have my gratitude as well.

The biggest thanks go to my husband Colby and my son Cade. You guys are my happiness.

All rights reserved. No part of this ebook may be re-sold, given away, or reproduced in any other manner without the written permission of the publisher.

Table of Contents

Acknowledgments 3
Chapter One 6
Chapter Two 10
Chapter Three 18
Chapter Four 26
Chapter Five 33
Chapter Six 36
Chapter Seven 38
Chapter Eight 43
Chapter Nine 48
Chapter Ten 55
Chapter Eleven 61
Chapter Twelve 68
Chapter Thirteen 72
Chapter Fourteen 77
Chapter Fifteen 84
Chapter Sixteen 89
Chapter Seventeen 96
Chapter Eighteen 98
Chapter Nineteen 100
Chapter Twenty 105
Chapter Twenty-One 113
Chapter Twenty-Two 121
Chapter Twenty-Three 124
Chapter Twenty-Four 132
Chapter Twenty-Five 135
Chapter Twenty-Six 137
Chapter Twenty-Seven 142
Chapter Twenty-Eight 147
Chapter Twenty-Nine 149
Chapter Thirty 153
Chapter Thirty-One 155
Chapter Thirty-Two 156
Chapter Thirty-Three 158
Chapter Thirty-Four 160
En Mi Viejo San Juan/In My Old San Juan 162
Hello, Reader! 165
About the Author 166
Other Titles by Cyndia Rios-Myers: 167

Chapter One

Vacation, by definition, is temporary. I'd not looked that up, but I could imagine that vacations are vacations because they are meant to be recreational, marked periods-of-time away from home. And I was away from home.

Once upon a time, Puerto Rico had been home. At the age of ten, I moved there from Boston, Massachusetts, with my parents and my brother. It was a culture shock, of course, but I got used to it. I made peace with it. I began to thrive in it.

But then I went and let Anibal Robles get a little too freaky with me. I got pregnant with my son, Hector Robles, so I married Anibal. I had to quit my job as a police officer and had to move to Chicago, Illinois, to try to make my marriage work.

It didn't work. For twelve years, I stuck with the non-working marriage. I built a thick-sized, angry, bitter shell around me. I divorced Anibal and moved out on my own. I became a maid, and I made a little money. But then I lost my son and most of my will to live.

My stagnant life changed when I watched a video I was *not* supposed to watch. I got kind of close with a couple of cops, made enemies with my old boss, and I started a private maid service. A friend of mine required some sleuthing assistance; I brushed off my detective skills and gave her a hand. All in all, I'd shaken off the angry, bitter shell that I'd built around myself.

In my present moment, I was happy. Especially because I was taking a break from a brutal Chicago winter while spending time with my beautiful family in Arecibo, Puerto Rico.

But it was a vacation; I reminded myself. I had to go home, and soon. Still, for that moment, I was going to live my vacation dreams. I was going to sink my teeth in it and savor it and prolong the flavor for as long as I could.

Speaking of savoring good things, that was what I was doing to the slice of pepperoni pizza I was eating. I was at Tony's Pizza with Rafy, his wife Wanda, and their twin sons, Julian and José.

"You could have this every week, Marta," said Rafael Morales Mercado. He stood at 5'11", was buff, as he lifted weights, and tan in a coffee-and-cream sort of way. Rafy was handsome. He always dressed well. In my opinion, he was probably a bit too coiffed. His head of dark hair looked too polished. It was part of his non-uniform uniform, though, and he was trying to send a message. Rafy was a good husband, a great dad, a police detective, and my stubborn, bossy, loud-mouthed older brother. I loved him dearly.

"You can live here. Have me and Wanda look out for you as well as *Mami* and *Papi*. You could hang out with your nephews. You could get away from Chicago - that dark walk-up you live in. Winters. Your crazy-ass old boss. The shady fucking lawyers at Smithers."

Rafy's tone was starting to get impassioned, though it hadn't started that way. Before his comment turned into a rant, it sounded hopeful, helpful, and kind. I sipped my soda while I waited for my brother's talk to turn into a tirade.

I didn't have to wait long.

"No! Marta isn't coming home. Why would she do that? Why would she do something so sensible, like moving close to her family? No! ¡Marta Morales lo sabe todo!"

I let out a breath. Even Rafy's wife, Wanda, rolled her eyes. I honestly wished I knew everything. Rafy seemed to believe I did.

"Great performance art," I said as I set down my soda and reached for another slice of pizza.

My sister-in-law, momentarily forgetting her loyalty to her husband, let out a snicker.

"Oh! So you laugh at me?! Do you think I'm funny? Do I make you laugh because I care?"

"Calm down," I said, my patience gone. "You aren't Joe Pesci, and this isn't Goodfellas."

Wanda laughed out loud, as did my nephews, though I was sure that they did not understand the movie reference. Thankfully, Rafy thought I was funny, too.

"You are lucky that it was funny."

I gave him a genuine smile. "Thank you. I'm here all week. Or...just under a week, which is when I go back to Chicago."

Rafy let out a breath. "So, you're going back."

"I have to," I said as I pulled on a long stretch of yummy, oily cheese. "I have clients. I have rent. I have bills. I have to pay into Social Security."

"You could have rent and bills here, too."

"Ha, ha," I said. Rafy could be funny, too.

"You want to get back to your side gig," he whispered.

"That, too. That can make me money in a way that doesn't break my back."

"It could break your neck, though."

"I like sleuthing, Rafy. It is fulfilling. I am going to do my best not to get hurt doing this."

My brother let out a breath and looked at his wife. "You're a psychologist. What do you think about this shit?"

"¡Papi dijo una mala palabra!" Julian said as he laughed.

"You got me! I said a cuss word. I will put two dollars," Rafy said as he reached for his wallet, "in the cuss jar if you say that again, but in English."

Julian looked away.

"You boys need to speak more English," their mother insisted. "Here am I with a big accent, and I speak English. You have almost no accent!"

José sighed. "I like money," he enunciated. "Daddy said a bad word. Now: give me my money."

I laughed, but Rafy shook his head. "No. The deal was for Julian. It is only one dollar for Spanish. Two for English."

My poor nephew blushed profusely.

"How about I sweeten the pot?" I asked. I pulled my wallet from my purse and took a five-dollar-bill from it. Both brothers' brown eyes widened, and Wanda laughed out loud.

"Julian? Your Dad said a bad word. Is it worth *seven* dollars?"

"Yes! My Dad said a bad word!" he excitedly said.

"Yes!" Rafy cheered as he high-fived both his sons and handed them two dollar bills. I gave them the five-dollar bill they'd earned.

"Keep swearing, Daddy. I like money. I like Titi Marta's money," said José. Julian echoed the sentiment in Spanish.

My brother's expression changed fast. "You'd take advantage of your Titi like that? Of me? Because we want you to learn another language and improve your chances of success?"

Rafy could go from cold to hot super-fast. I said nothing, though, as his sons and their discipline was his business. There was also more to Rafy's regulation than good manners.

Back when Rafy was 13, and we were still living in Boston, he'd gone down a wrong path, which had been the cause of our move to Puerto Rico. Rafy wanted to ensure that his sons would not make the same choices he had.

"Sorry, Dad," said Julian.

"Thank you. Now, apologize to your Titi," Rafy demanded.

"Sorry, Titi Marta," my twin nephews said.

I smiled in response. "Thank you."

Wanda let out a breath and opened her purse. "Alright. I know there are only two video games. Here are the quarters. Go play."

"*Uno se cansa de Street Fighter*," grumbled one of them.

Their boredom with the fighting game did not deter them from snatching up their mother's quarters, though. When they were a few tables away from us, Wanda looked at me.

"This private detective business is good for your mental and emotional health. Good for your wallet. But you have to be careful!"

"I know. I don't take my safety for granted," I whispered.

Rafy let out a breath. "I'm still keeping an eye out for that cunt Maria," he confided.

Only a few weeks ago, my old boss Maria held a gun against the back of my head. I could still feel the cold kiss of the metal on my scalp.

"I won't go on about it anymore," Rafy said. "I just hope that if you get in over your head, that you get out and let someone know."

"I will, Rafy."

He nodded. "Okay. I gotta go and kick these effers asses again. They think that they can take their old man at Street Fighter."

Wanda and I laughed as we watched Rafy head towards Julian and José. The boys cheered at the sight of their Dad but jeered as soon as they heard his blustering.

"I never get tired of seeing him have fun with the boys," Wanda said.

I had a bite of my pizza before speaking. "Do you think Rafy would have been that devoted and excited, had you two not had fertility issues?"

My sister-in-law shrugged. "He would have been devoted. But this excited? Probably not," she said as she shook her head. "He is grateful for the boys. Especially because he knows how short life can sometimes be."

Wanda was talking about Hector. I missed so much about him. He wasn't just a life lesson or a cautionary tale, though - he'd been a living, speaking, fallible, breathing being. I didn't snap at my sister-in-law for her words, though. I knew she meant well.

Trying to distract myself from tears, I looked around the restaurant. Tony's Pizza was renowned as the best pizza place in Arecibo, and probably most of Puerto Rico. My parents had been bringing Rafy and me there for years. We continued the tradition with our own children.

The front side of the restaurant wasn't much to look at. Tony's faced State Road #2 - a bustling artery that fronted the entire northern coast of the island. The backside was a different story - huge windows featured panoramic views of the Atlantic Ocean.

I let out a breath and immersed myself in the beautiful view inside the pizzeria, too—my brother playing video games with my nephews, and my awesome sister-in-law sitting across from me.

"So. How is work going?" I asked of her.

Wanda smiled. "Wonderfully. Let me tell you about it."

Happily, I got lost in the conversation and the moment as well.

Chapter Two

The guest experience at my parents' home was decidedly different than the one at my brother's place. My parents' house offered my childhood bedroom and the odd comfort and surreal nature that was sleeping in the room I'd slept in so many years passed. The food was great there, too. However, expectations came with my stay. My folks wanted me to go EVERYWHERE with them - to visit every family member related to me by blood, and to go to the supermarket with them. To with them to pay the water bill out in town. It was tedious and boring.

Staying at my brother's house involved 24/7 availability of aunt and nephew playtime, which I didn't mind too much. It was the constant bickering and yelling that took getting used to. Also, my sister-in-law was not so good a cook. However, my brother and sister-in-law allowed me my freedom. Wanda would let me borrow her car so that I could drive myself around and do the things I wanted to do. I had terrific nighttime conversations on the porch with my brother, his wife, and their neighbors.

The solution to both problems was to get a vacation rental and pay for a rental car. However, due to my lack of vacation funds, I was at the mercy of my hosts.

I was quiet one night as I sat on the porch with my brother and Wanda. For a second, I remembered my ex-husband Anibal. I thought about the time when our marriage had been younger and more hopeful; I was a cop in Arecibo, and he was a bookkeeper in the neighboring town of Hatillo. We had our infant son, Hector. We had good times and good conversations with our neighbors. Family - his and my own - were everywhere. Had we stayed in Puerto Rico with Hector, maybe we could have found a way to stay together.

But, like a song once said, that was water under a bridge that had burned long ago.

I shook myself from my reverie and looked at my brother.

"You are almost outta here," he said.

I sighed. "Yeah. Three more days."

"You are already outta here in your head," he said as he pointed to his own.

"Look at you philosophizing," I teased.

He scoffed. "Nah. Just observing."

I nodded. "No. I remembered the past. Good times with Anibal, believe it or not."

Rafy laughed. "I find that hard to believe. Not that you didn't have good times with him, but that you would reflect on that."

"It's not reflection; it's memory. I don't ignore the fact that I used to be happy with Anibal. I'd be lying if I denied that. How can I live in reality if I lie to myself about what came before?"

"Who's philosophizing now?" Rafy asked.

I laughed. "You got me."

"How is Anibal?" asked Wanda.

I let out a breath. "Doing well professionally and financially. Anibal doesn't hate me; he's let his assistant be my professional advisor free-of-cost. He's still married to the *puta*, but I think they're good. I think his kids are good, too."

"How about Waleska? Has she reached out yet? Told you about your grandson?" asked Rafy.

I let out a slow, shaking breath as I thought about my daughter-in-law. She'd cut herself out of my life when she'd begun to mourn Hector. In the process, she kept my grandson Adan from me. It stung.

"Waleska's keeping her distance, still."

"It's been almost three years, Marta. Don't you think she should have gotten past mourning enough to let you see your grandson?" Rafy asked.

"Yes, Rafy! I do. But I don't know what to do here. Do I force myself on her? Do I try to fight to see Adan? I don't know!"

Wanda tilted her head as she faced her husband. "She has a point. It is a mess."

"It isn't," Rafy argued. "In Illinois, grandparents can get court-ordered visitation."

I stared at my brother. "Really?"

"Yeah. I looked into it. But I would suggest that you first approach Wanda in a friendly manner. If things get ugly, then hire a lawyer. That is Hector's son. You know he would have wanted you to be a part of his son's life."

I swallowed at tears and looked away. I was not ready to have so emotional a conversation. Still, the information provided by my brother was valuable. The thought of facing my daughter-in-law put some fear in me. I didn't understand why, though. I'd encountered criminal lawyers, stalkers, and even my old boss, who still wanted to kill me.

"Okay. Okay. I am going to start pulling at that thread. I don't want to discuss it any further, though."

"Okay," Rafy said before sipping his beer.

The next morning held Sunday mass at my family's regular parish. Thankfully, I remembered the prayers in Spanish. I wasn't sure if I'd memorized the prayers in English. Another thing to add to the Catholic guilt file.

The priest's monotone homily gave wings to my thoughts, and I took the time to reflect on my church attendance. I wasn't a regular church-goer—no good reason for that. I wasn't mad at God because my son died. I even owned up to my role in my divorce. I figured that my lack of attendance was owed to shame, as I could not receive communion. I'd married Anibal in the church, but upon divorcing, we'd not gotten an annulment. I guess that meant he was living in sin. Save for a failed date with a Spanish interpreter, I'd not seen a man (on a personal level) in years. Maybe I *could* receive the Eucharist.

I thought about the two handsome Chicago detectives, and what their religious affiliations might be. Detective Connelly was probably Catholic. Detective Kostas might have been Greek Orthodox, which was kind of Catholic. Did the detectives go to Sunday masses? Did they pray a lot? Back when I was a cop, I'd always carry a pocket rosary. I stopped praying it upon moving to Chicago, though. I wondered where that pocket rosary had gotten to.

A flying elbow to my arm delivered by my mother alerted me that it was time to stand up and do some more group praying. I got the stink-eye from some parishioners when I didn't get in line for the Eucharist. I let out a breath and got on the kneeler, doing my best to pray for the catty people who weren't minding their own business. I prayed for myself, too.

After mass, we made our way out of the church and to the fried food kiosk by the rectory. God forgive me, but the deep-fried smells might have been the highlight of that morning's mass.

"*No comulgaste,*" my Mom admonished.

My sweet mother was starting to chafe me. The vacation had gone on long enough; my patience was shot, and I let it show.

"No, Mom," I said, unable to keep the reproving tone from my voice. "I am divorced. I have not received an annulment. I cannot receive the Eucharist."

"In God's eyes, you are still married."

I groaned. "But not in Anibal's eyes. Who knows what his lecherous eyes are gazing at right now?"

"You just left the church!"

"Yeah, I know," I said. "And I am ready for an *empanadilla de pizza* and some soda. Maybe an *alcapurria* if I have room."

"I am trying to talk to you!"

"Yeah, and I'm trying to eat."

I left my mother and headed to the kiosk that did have both *empanadillas de pizza* AND *alcapurrias*. I beamed as I paid for the deep-fried pizza and ground beef/plantain fritters. Still smiling, I carried my fat-laden goodies and soda to a picnic table on the other side of the kiosk.

There, I saw my nephews. I did not see my brother or sister-in-law with them. Elbow-deep in fried food, they seemed unconcerned about their absent parents. I was about to join them.

"Where are your parents?" I asked.

"*Hablando con abuelo. ¿Porque tú no nos habla en español?*" asked Julian.

Satisfied that my nephews were not being neglected, I answered the question posed to me.

"I don't have to speak to you in Spanish, because I'm an adult. Your father and your mother want you to learn English. And frankly, you guys are lazy about it."

"What does 'frankly' mean?" asked Jose.

"It means being honest. Now, it's time to eat. *Buen provecho*," I said to them.

"*Buen provecho*," they answered in kind.

Soon, we reverently devoured our fried foods. Twenty minutes later held me moving my luggage from my brother's car trunk to my father's.

"I am going to have to rent my own car next time."

"Why would you waste money like that?" asked Rafy.

"Because I feel like a latchkey kid! I'm a grown woman!"

"Then quit pouting like a baby," he countered.

I let out a slow, calming breath.

"What's a 'latchkey kid?'" asked Wanda of Rafy.

"It's what parents do to their school-aged kids when they don't love them enough - they make them go home alone from school to their cold and lonely houses."

I scoffed. "That's mean."

"Never said I was nice," Rafy said.

I rolled my eyes. "Mom and Dad; can we get to the *comida* already?"

"Sure," said Mom. "I can't imagine that you'll still be hungry for the family picnic after all the food you ate."

I let out another calming breath. When that didn't work, I let out another. Like a teenager of old, I sulked in the backseat of my parents' car - until I remembered that I was forty and that my time in Puerto Rico was limited.

"There's going to be slush all over the place," I said as I looked out my window to the passing greenery.

"I don't miss that," said Dad. "I miss the cold. I miss seeing the snow on the grass," he said in his accent. "I do not miss shoveling snow or driving in it."

"I don't have to shovel where I live, thank God. Doña Justa hires that out."

"How is your landlady doing?" Asked Mom.

"Good. Doña Justa wants me to bring her some *pasteles*."

Mom nodded. "We'll send some home with you."

"Yum," I said in answer.

Twenty minutes later held us in Esperanza - a country neighborhood high in the southern mountain range of Arecibo. Upon parking, I saw my mother's sisters, and I smiled. I hugged my cousins and their kids, too. I smiled even wider when a cousin handed me a cold Medalla beer.

"Now it's a party," I said to my English-speaking cousin Almira.

Almira laughed out loud. "Sometimes, it's the only way to get through these things," she whispered.

Surprising my Mom and myself I found more room for food. I ate roast pork and rice with chickpeas. I then had some more pork.

"Keep stuffing your face like that, and you'll have to get a seatbelt extender," Rafy said to me in passing.

"Get bent!" I replied.

He shrugged and kept walking.

My brother's ribbing marked the last amusing exchange of that afternoon. Everyone wanted to know how I liked being a maid - aunt after aunt, cousin after cousin, and family friend after family friend.

"You like that? Really? Oh! God bless you!" condescended one.

"I hate cleaning!" added an aunt. "But you love it. Good for you," she said with a smile.

I forced a smile and thanked her before walking away. An uncle stopped me to give me his unreserved opinion. "You have nothing to be ashamed of. Nothing! Being a maid is honest work. Good for you!"

Lord, help me. I told that uncle that my cell phone was vibrating in my pocket and asked to be excused.

"¿Te llega señal por aca arriba?" he questioned.

My uncle was skeptical that I was able to get a cell phone signal so high in the mountains. And for good reason, as I was lying. Still, I shrugged and walked to a spot where no one else was standing.

I leaned on a palm tree and took a breath. The mountain air smelled so fresh, as did the flowers. Everything was so green - the wild grasses, the bushes, the palms, and the hills that surrounded us.

"This is nice," I whispered.

I felt like I knew the land, and that I knew the people, too. For generations going back hundreds of years, my ancestors walked the mountain paths and roads. I shared some of those ancestors with some of the people around me. If we didn't share ancestors, our ancestors rubbed elbows with each other.

I couldn't live there, though. I had an apartment in Chicago. Clients that I liked. A job that I was good at, and a side gig that was very exciting. Also, there were a couple of very friendly gentlemen I wanted to get to know.

Puerto Rico held family - so much of it. Great food, good times, and great conversations. Still, it could not give me what Chicago offered.

My Mom joined me. "Why are you away from everyone else?" she asked.

"I'm trying to get away from the condescending people." I told her what they'd said. She shrugged it off.

"They mean well."

"I guess," I said as I rolled my eyes.

"Hang out here for a minute and then come back. You won't have this in Chicago."

"I know," I drew out, feeling like a sulky teenager all over again.

"Also, I might have a lead for you on some private detective work."

I shoved off the palm tree and stared at her. "What?"

She smiled and nodded before walking away. I followed. I had to drink another beer and listen to three more condescending family members before my Mom introduced me to a middle-aged woman I'd never met.

"Marta - this is Doña Elena Matos Boria. She is my second cousin, twice removed from your grandfather's side of the family that came from the town of Lares."

I didn't have a pad of paper or a pencil with me to chart that relationship. Thankfully, all I had to remember was the woman's name.

"*Hola, Doña Elena. Mucho gusto en conocerle,*" I said as I stood up to shake the middle-aged woman's hand.

"Nice to meet you, too, Marta. Your mother tells me that you are a detective."

I shook my head. "I can't use that title, being that I am unlicensed. I like to call myself a sleuth. What can I do for you?" I asked.

Doña Elena indicated a bench by a tree. Understanding her desire for privacy, I accompanied her there. She sat down and smiled.

"Do you want to know something amazing?"

I shrugged. "Sure."

"The human body - it is God's greatest invention. It is amazing!"

I nodded slowly, wondering where Doña Elena's conversation was going. "Of course."

"Yes. Did you know that something amazing lives inside of each one of us?"

Dear, me. Was she doing to talk about speaking in tongues? Didn't she know that I was Catholic and not Pentecostal?

"What specifically?" I asked.

Doña Elena clapped. "I knew I would surprise you. There is this wonderful thing called DNA. It is the blueprint of everything we are."

I stared at her in shock. Did this woman think that I'd never heard of DNA?

"It is surprising," she said, misinterpreting my confusion for ignorance. "Let me tell you all about it!"

Dear God. Doña Elena must have thought that I did not have basic cable, access to newspapers, skipped high school, and was stupid about pregnancy and childbirth.

"DNA can be found in so many parts of our body! Our blood, our saliva, our skin, and our teeth! Even in our poop!"

That wasn't exactly true. The human body did not waste DNA on excrement; if it existed in there, there would only be trace amounts. However, the DNA of the animals we ate might be found there.

I did not say any of this to Elena, though, as she might be a paying customer. Also, I did not want to reveal that I'd learned about poo DNA through a cop show.

So, I sat there and listened to Elena re-educate me on DNA. I interrupted the unsolicited lecture when I realized that she was trying to talk about DNA in menstrual blood.

"Elena - this is stimulating information. However, I want to know what this has to do with my investigating skills."

She nodded. "Of course. Well. Have you ever heard of at-home DNA test kits?"

Before I could stop her, Doña Elena launched into everything I'd ever seen on daytime TV, Facebook, Judge Judy, or the junk email folder of my inbox.

"I tested myself," she announced. "No surprises there. Mostly Spanish DNA. Some Portuguese and Italian. Taino blood and Africa blood, too. And blood from Finland, if you can believe that!" she added.

I had no humor left, though, and even less patience.

"Doña Elena, as much as I would love to talk about these...exciting test results, I am here with my parents and my brother Rafy. I think he's ready to go. Don't tell anyone," I said in a lower tone of voice, "but Rafy has irritable bowel syndrome," I said.

Her eyes widened. "Wow! That must be stress from being a police officer."

"Yes," I nodded. "Rafy's on the gassy side. But please don't tell anyone," I reiterated.

"Of course, of course. Your secret is safe with me," Doña Elena said.

"How about I meet you in town tomorrow? We can have donuts and coffee while we discuss this further."

She beamed. "Yes. That sounds lovely. How about we meet at *Los Cidrines* at 10 a.m.?"

"That works for me. Could I have your phone number?"

Fifteen minutes later held me driving away from the mountains while in the backseat of my father's car.

"Did your mother tell you that Doña Elena likes to talk?" Dad asked.

"No, Dad. She did *not*," I drew out.

Mom shrugged. "So what? She likes to talk. Conversation doesn't hurt anyone."

Mom felt the need to converse further, as she turned around and faced me from where she sat in the front seat.

"It wasn't so bad, was it?"

"I guess not," I said.

"Also, she's buried two husbands. Maybe three," Mom added as she smiled.

"I don't know that I would smile at that."

"Doña Elena collects Social Security AND two pensions, and she owns three houses. She's loaded. So, when she talks, people listen. She mentioned to me that there was someone in Chicago that she was trying to find, so I mentioned you."

"Oh."

"You see? I am looking out for you, Marta."

"Thanks, Mom. I appreciate that."

Feeling validated and appreciated (and rightly so), Mom turned around in her seat.

Back in my parents' townhome and in my childhood bedroom, I looked at my cell phone. It did not get a signal in the mountains. I had four missed calls and two text messages.

"Yikes," I said.

They were all from Melissa Bollinger - my cleaning client, first sleuthing customer, and my new buddy. The fact that she called four times made me disregard the texts. I called her directly.

"Marta!" she said. "Are you okay?"

"I'm fine! How are you?"

"I've tried calling you over the past few hours, but worried when I didn't get you."

I looked around my bedroom and chuckled. "Well. No hurricanes have hit. No earthquakes, and no political unrest - at the moment," I qualified. "Because Puerto Ricans love to protest."

Melissa laughed out loud. "How's it been?"

I let out a sigh. "Good. Nice. Warm. And I'm getting fatter because I am eating all deep-fried foods. At this point, I'd probably have some deep-fried coffee."

"That exists already!"

"Of course, it does."

"Anyway, I am calling to let you know that I can't pick you up from the airport. I am so sorry about that! One of our blue chips invested badly, and things aren't looking good for them. Niels is unhappy," she whispered. "We are leaving for Brazil tomorrow evening."

"I'm sorry about the blue-chip, but I am okay on getting my own ride."

"I feel bad! You are my only good friend out here, and friends pick up friends from the airport."

I laughed. "Friends don't put friends through the O'Hare experience. At rush hour, or any time in Chicago. I'll call an Uber."

"I'm so sorry," she apologized.

"Hey! You go and enjoy Brazil, alright? I can't wait to hear about it."

She laughed. "You are the best, Marta."

"So are you," I replied.

After a quick goodbye, I got off the phone. I was out a ride, but I was still tight with my friend. It was another reason why I looked forward to getting back to Chicago.

Chapter Three

Oddly enough, I was looking forward to meeting up with Doña Elena. Perhaps it was owed to my boredom. Maybe it was owed to the fact that my Mom went back to talking to me like I was a teenager.

It was probably because I was intrigued. Who did this bored, monied, condescending woman want to locate? How much was she willing to pay? I was about to find out, I knew.

"Look," Mom said to me. "I am about to pay the water bill in town," she said as she parked the car on the street by the plaza. "Just come with me. You can make it to your appointment on time."

"No," I said as I unbuckled my seatbelt and opened the door.

"It will only take a minute," she pleaded.

"Not even you believe that. Also, I want to walk through the pueblo."

"There's nothing to see. Everything is closed."

I let out a sad breath. "I know. I know that the Arecibo of the late eighties and early nineties is gone. Still, I want to see the skeleton. It's so pretty, still."

"Fine," she said, finally relenting. "I will meet you at the *Cidrines*."

"Sounds good to me."

I walked down the Avenida Jose de Diego. My wooden-heeled slides sounded loud as they struck the cobbled streets. I stared at the abandoned storefronts that hugged either side of the pedestrian-only avenue. I recalled the businesses that used to be there - Woolworth, Mocega, Baker Shoes, Butler Shoes, and an ice-cream store. Some new businesses had taken occupancy of the locales - mostly restaurants.

The Arecibo I was seeing, and the Arecibo of my youth were vastly different. People used to live in apartments over the storefronts. Girls and boys and young women and men dashed from store to store while wearing their school uniforms. Public cars - Puerto Rico's answer to mass public transportation - parked all around the plaza, picking up and dropping off shoppers and errand runners from their neighborhoods to the pueblo and back again. People of all ages congregated on corners to talk. The cathedral's church bells alerted people of the time. Now, not so much.

Malls changed things for Puerto Rican towns, and so did the faltering economy. I was sure that if Puerto Rico had not been a U.S. territory and if Puerto Rico's people did not have U.S. Citizenship, that maybe most would have stayed.

Thoughts of ghosts and times gone disappeared just as soon as I caught the scent of freshly-baked bread. I entered the bakery and quickly spotted Doña Elena. She was seated in the back, waving at me as I walked her way.

At my approach, Doña Elena stood up and greeted me with a cheek-to-cheek air kiss.

"I am so glad you could make it," she said.

I smiled. "Of course. I was very intrigued by our conversation yesterday. I cannot wait to hear more, but first, would you mind if I go to the counter to get myself some pastries and coffee?"

I moved to stand up but was stopped by a hand. "There's no need. I already got you some coffee and a *pastelillito*."

I pasted a smile on my face as I accepted the cup of lukewarm coffee. I hid a frown as I took the guava-paste filled pastry I was not fond of.

"How considerate of you. Thank you."

She nodded in acceptance. After a swallow or two of the not-so-bad coffee, I pulled out a pad and a pen.

"Now. Tell me everything. What you think is relevant and what you think is irrelevant. I want to hear all of it."

Doña Elena beamed and looked very pretty. I could see why she'd landed two husbands.

"Look at how well prepared you are! I knew I was right about hiring you."

"Well, you haven't hired me yet, as you don't know my rates. Still, I'd like to hear you out and see if there's anything I can do for you. Once I do that, I can determine a preliminary scope-of-work and can then come up with a price for my services."

She nodded. "Yes. Okay. Like I told you, I did the DNA test. Have you ever had one done?"

I banked my irritation. "I've not. Are the tests difficult?"

"No. Not at all. I will pay for a DNA test for you so that you can see what it is all about."

I thought about that for a moment. "That's a good idea, Doña Elena."

She smiled. "Okay. Here is the story..."

Two cups of coffee, a glazed donut plus a sugar-covered donut, one hour and one impatient mother later, I'd come up with a price.

"I don't negotiate on prices, Doña Elena. I don't do discounts. The work I do is sometimes dangerous. I am not even sure it is completely legal. What I know is that I can get the goods for you. I won't scam you, and I won't overcharge you."

"What is your price?"

"I'll need a good-faith deposit of five hundred dollars. Depending on how long it takes me to get results, the rest of it will be between one thousand to fifteen hundred dollars."

I heard my Mom coughing from the table behind me, presumably over my going rates. I ignored her. Doña Elena paled a bit, herself.

"I imagine that it will take me about six weeks to get the results you want. For my fee, you can call me for weekly updates. I can call you. If I cannot get you the results you want, I will not charge you for anything beyond the deposit, which I will keep."

Doña Elena silently stared at me.

"I interpret your silence as hesitance. That is okay; it's reasonable," I added as I sat forward on my seat. "I am not cheap. Also, you are paying for answers that you might not like. I would advise this: take some time to think about it. You can call me on my cell once you've made a decision. Or don't call me at all. I'll interpret that as you not wanting to proceed."

Doña Elena nodded. "You've given me a lot to think about. I will call you this evening with my decision."

"Okay. Just in case you want to do this, I only accept cash."

Doña Elena's face screwed up a bit. "I understand."

I gave her my sleuth phone number and then thanked her for the coffee, pastries, and her company. I stood up and joined my Mom.

"Alright, Mom. Next stop: Hatillo."

"Why?" she dramatically asked.

"You know why; to go to the deep-fried fritters store. Gotta take some back to Chicago."

Looking put-upon, Mom followed me out the bakery and back up the Avenida José de Diego, where we rehashed what Arecibo used to be.

A few hours later found me back in my childhood bedroom. Looking at the darkening sky, I was reminded that my time in Puerto Rico was coming to an end. The next few hours would pass like minutes, I knew. I'd have dinner with my parents as well as my brother and his family. We would discuss our days and what was to come. And then, the inevitable questions would come.

"So, when are you coming back?" asked Rafy over dinner.

I shrugged. "I don't know the answer to that."

"But you have more money coming in now, right?" He asked before reaching for another fried pork chop. "With your side job, I mean."

I gave him the stink-eye in warning. While he knew that I'd been held at gunpoint, my parents did not. I intended to keep it that way.

I let out a breath. "Well...I need a confirmed gig, which means money. I need more for savings - not just travel. Also, I've spent money since I've been here."

"On what? You haven't been paying for room, board, or food," he countered.

"Dental work, jerk!"

"Hey! No rude talk at my table," Mom said.

"I am trying to be nice, mom, but there's only so much patience I can have when Rafy acts like an idiot."

"Does idiot mean *idiota*, Dad?" asked José of my idiotic brother.

Rafy let out a slow breath. "Yes, José. That's what 'idiot' means, but we don't use that word."

"Titi Marta called you an idiot," said Julian.

Immediately I was ashamed. "Julian and José? I should not have called your Dad that. I am sorry you heard me say that to him."

"Doesn't sound like an apology," said Rafy.

I set my fork down and rubbed my temples, trying to stop the headache that was coming my way.

"Marta: you aren't used to big dinners anymore, are you?" asked my typically-reserved father.

I groaned. "Well, Dad. You are right in that I live alone. I typically eat dinner all by myself. And it is lonely. But the truth is that I am having a hard time with our family dynamic. I'm older now, and it's harder to hide."

Everyone stopped eating and stared at me instead.

"What do you mean?" asked my Mom.

I let out a sigh. "Rafy is abrasive and domineering, Mom. You overlook that because that's rewarded behavior here. Dad overlooks it, too. You pity me because you think I live a small life. And I do," I said as my voice caught. "I am still walking out of the prison I put myself in. I like where my life is going. I am trying to be nicer and at peace. But here, at this table again, I feel like I have to put my armor back on, and I don't want to do that. I just want to have a good meal with you all, because I don't know when I'll make it back here again."

I didn't mean to upset anyone, but I did. Mom swallowed at something in her throat. Wanda wiped her eyes, and Rafy pushed his chair out before walking out of the dining room.

"Look at what you did," Mom said. "You made your brother upset."

I shook my head and stood up. "Dad? I am taking your car."

"You know where the keys are," he said.

"Where are you going?" Mom asked.

"None of your business," I barked.

I grabbed my purse from the couch and then took my father's keys. I passed my brother, who sat on the porch.

"Where are you going?" he asked.

"None of your business, either!"

I got in the driver's side of my Dad's car and turned it on. Seconds later, the passenger side door opened. My stupid brother sat down and strapped himself in.

"What are you doing?" I angrily asked.

"Maybe I want to get the fuck out of here, too," was his answer.

Grumbling, I turned the car on and backed out of the driveway. I drove down the hill that left my parents' neighborhood and revealed the ocean. It was so gorgeous during that time of the evening.

"This time's a magical one," I said to Rafy.

He nodded but said nothing. Fifteen minutes later held us parked at a floral shop in town. I walked in and politely requested two dozen red roses.

"*Dame dos docenas adicionales, por favor,*" my brother politey requested.

Rafy paid for his roses and tried to pay for mine, too.

"No, but thanks," I said to him.

Ten minutes later held us at the graveyard by the cathedral. I smiled just as soon as I saw my son's headstone.

"Hi, Papi," I said as I touched Hector's picture.

I'd been there three times in the past week and a half. I took the older flowers from their pots and set the new ones in.

"Here. Let me put the old ones in Tio Jose's pots," said Rafy.

The older roses made it to the flower pots belonging to the uncle we'd lost in Vietnam. He'd passed before we were born, but we never forgot to stop and say hi.

I sat down next to my son's headstone and stared at his picture. Rafy sat next to me.

"I come here every week," he said.

"I know."

"Every Friday evening," he said as he cleared his throat. "Mom still comes twice a week. Anibal's parents come every other week or so."

"He's not forgotten," I said with a half-smile.

"Wouldn't it have been easier if he were buried in Chicago?"

I shook my head. "No. It's like I said before; he has no ancestors buried in the U.S. Here, his ancestors can look out for him."

"You know, he doesn't need anyone looking out for him anymore, right?" Rafy asked.

I let a breath out. "It's a mom thing. I'll always worry."

I looked at my son's handsome face, which had been beautifully etched on his headstone. Hector had my eyes and nose, but Anibal's smile and his hairline.

"How do you think he'd be right now, had he lived?"

"Goodness. Probably still injured. On the outside and the inside. Maybe he'd still be married. Maybe with more kids beyond Adan? Maybe divorced," I said on a sigh. "He and Waleska were going through some rough times before he passed."

"Do you think he'd be living with you again?"

I nodded. "Probably. But, maybe Hector would have surprised me. Maybe he would have gone back to college and gotten that degree in accounting. Maybe he would have found a way to handle the depression and have a satisfying home life at the same time."

My brother nodded. "He'd be proud of you, you know. Starting your own business. Having fun again."

"I hope so."

Rafy was quiet for a bit. "I don't mean to push you so much, you know? I'm an asshole. I usually get away with it, but you call me on it. I am grateful for that, believe it or not. Wanda and Mami deserve better from me."

I shrugged. "Well, you are an asshole, but probably a nicer one than the other assholes on this island."

"I'll own that. I just hope that you know that you can come back."

"Thanks."

On that sweet but somber note, we headed back to our parents' house. After my parents went to bed, I called Chicago.

"Hello, Marta," said a voice that excited me.

I could not help the smile that split my face. "Hello. I am calling because I need a small favor. Actually, it's not small," I said as I blushed and paced my childhood bedroom. "It's kind of big. Sort of."

"Let's hear it."

"Is there any chance you might be able to pick me up at the airport tomorrow afternoon? My friend Melissa was supposed to pick me up, but she had an emergency trip to Brazil-"

"What airline?" he asked.

His volume was low, and I wondered if he was with someone else. Embarrassed, I changed my mind.

"You know what? Never mind. I don't mean to interrupt you like this. I can get an Uber."

"Why are you being weird?"

"Because you are whispering on the phone. I'm going to hang up now."

"I'm on the clock, Marta, and I'm waiting to meet someone - work-related. I can pick you up tomorrow," he insisted.

"Are you sure?"

"Yes," he groaned. "What airline and what time?"

"American. I'll land at two p.m. I'll be outside of the baggage claim. But if you can't make it, I can just call-"

"I'll be there. I said I would." His tone was a bit sharp.

"You know what? Never mind. I can get an Uber."

He groaned. "I want to pick you up, okay? It's been a long day here, Marta. A few long days here. Nights, too. I welcome the opportunity to see you. Please, let me pick you up."

"Okay, but if you change your mind-"

"I'll be there. I gotta go now."

"Okay. Good night. And thank you," I meekly said.

"Thank you, Marta. Fly safe. I'll see you tomorrow."

"Okay."

I hung up the phone and let out a moan. "I shouldn't have called him!" I whined as I flopped on my bed.

My bedroom door opened. "Who did you call?" asked my Mom.

"What are you doing awake?" I asked as I sat up.

"Who were you on the phone with?"

"How is that any of your business?"

"You are my daughter, and I have a right to know."

I shook my head. "Well, I am not telling you, Mom. Just because you eavesdrop does not give you the right to my confidences."

She rolled her eyes and entered the room. "Fine. Don't tell me."

"Good."

I retrieved my suitcase from my closet and set it on the bed. I opened my dresser drawers and began to pack.

"I know it seems like Rafy is my favorite, but that isn't true."

"Lie," I tiredly said.

"I am not lying."

"Yes, you are. But I don't care, Mom. I get it. Rafy's your son and your firstborn."

She let out a breath. "Want to know something?"

"What?"

"I worry about you, and I pity you - just like you said earlier."

"I already knew that!" I said as I threw my lingerie into my case.

"But I am scared for you—more than I am scared for Rafy. Please try to understand my position. You are in a country far away, and I am scared."

I turned to face her. "Are you seriously trying to educate me on how it feels like to be scared for a child who is overseas? Are you REALLY doing that?" I loudly asked.

"Damn. Fuck," Mom cussed, surprising me. "I don't know how to say things to you sometimes. The words come out all wrong. They are organized in my head, but then I say them, and I hear how they sound," she said as her voice broke.

My anger evaporated. "I know, Mom. I know I'm hard."

"You are not, though. You are easy to understand, and I understand. I know that you chafe under the chauvinism that exists here. Because you are American, too - probably more American than Puerto Rican. I know you know this, but I'll say it anyway. Mothers never stop caring. Ever. I can't help but fuss over Rafy as I do. I cannot help it," she enunciated. "But trust me; I just want to see you happy and taken care of. Having you so far away where I can't take care of you is so hard for me."

I swallowed at tears. "I understand, Mom. It's okay."

"I don't see Chicago as you do. To you, it is a big exciting city full of activity and promise. To me, it is a sad gray place with mean people and bad winters. And then I picture you alone in your apartment, and I hate it. Because I want you to be happy."

I hugged her. "Thanks, Mom. I appreciate that. I appreciate you looking out for me."

She let out a shuddering breath and hugged me back. I let her go and went back to my packing.

"Will you promise me something?"

"That depends. What is it?"

"Will you quit the investigation stuff just as soon as it gets dangerous?"

Guilt-filled over what I'd kept from her, I swallowed audibly.

"I'll get out when things get bad," I said instead.

"Thank you."

I glanced at the clock and saw the late hour. My Mom was never up late.

"Why are you awake?"

She shrugged. "I got up to use the bathroom and heard you talking. I wanted to know what made you so nervous. Is it a man?"

"Yeah. It is. But, I'm not ready to talk about him. When I am, I will share. Okay?"

"Promise?"

"Yeah. Go to sleep, Mom."

"Okay. I love you."

"I love you, too, Mom."

I stared at my door long after she'd closed it. Our face-to-face argument went like a lot of our phone call arguments. First mild, then, angry and then ultimately kind and understanding. It was exhausting but real. I was thankful for it.

Chapter Four

Rafy came over for coffee the next morning, which was surprising. I took the time to inspect his work attire.

He was a detective, which meant he didn't have to wear a uniform. Still, his slacks, shirt, and tie indicated that he was a professional. The badge and gun strapped to his belt showed that he was the kind of professional you didn't want to cross.

"What are you doing here?" I asked.

He leaned down to accept a cheek-to-cheek kiss from me.

"Just came to get some coffee and gab before you fly out this morning."

"That's this morning, isn't it?" I said as I let out a breath.

"You can change your mind."

"Come on now."

Mom brought Rafy a cup of coffee and a Danish before sitting down at the dinner table with us. Dad was seated with us, too, but was reading a newspaper article, and quite intently.

"So. Is Doña Elena going to hire you?" Rafy asked before biting into his donut.

I let out a breath. "I haven't heard from Doña Elena yet, so I am thinking not, which is a shame. I was curious to see how the whole DNA/family member search would go. Plus, there was the money."

"The best part," my brother agreed.

Mom asked Rafy a question about Wanda; I diverted my attention to my father. His brow was furrowed as he stared at the paper.

"You've been reading the same thing for about ten minutes now," I said to him.

His eyes - laser-sharp - went from the paper to me.

"Yes," he said as he shook the paper. "Something isn't right here."

"What?" I asked, suddenly curious.

"A staff writer for the paper keeps reporting on the pastimes of a new widow. He talks about everything she buys with the insurance payout she received."

"Is it a gossip section of the paper? A social section? Editorial?"

"No. Not exactly. But that's not why this story matters."

"What do you think is going on?"

"Why are a widow's shopping trips newsworthy? That is the question."

My father looked like he already knew the answer to the question.

"Okay. I'll bite. Why is the writer reporting on this woman's spending habits?"

"Because the writer's been told to stop snooping in the mysterious diving death of her husband."

I stared at my Dad for a bit. Even Rafy stopped talking to our mother.

"Is it the widow out of Barceloneta?" my brother inquired.

Barceloneta was a smaller town to the east of Arecibo. It had a healthy economy owed to the pharmaceutical companies that had set up shop there.

"Yep," Dad answered.

Rafy leaned back in his seat. "I know who you're talking about. I'm pretty sure that the widow had her husband killed. The man left behind three sons for a previous marriage. But folks aren't talking. Cops have nothing to work with, save for suspicion."

I stared at my Dad for a bit. He looked like a school teacher waiting for someone to get the correct answer to a problem.

"Why is the writer so invested?" I asked.

"He probably wants justice," Rafy said.

The look in my Dad's eye said that he was looking for more.

"But that reporter better be careful. If the widow hired thugs to take care of her husband, she might hire thugs to take care of the reporter." Rafy said.

"She will probably get away with it on this plane," Mom said. "She will have to answer for her sins in the next plane, though."

Mom was right, but I was curious as to what Dad wanted us to uncover.

"What's the name of the reporter?"

"Wenceslao Santiago Vizcarrondo," Dad said as he smiled.

"That's not a common surname - the maternal one," I said.

Puerto Rico kept the Spanish convention of surnames; a child held their given name along with the father's surname followed by the mother's surname.

"It is not a common surname," Dad said.

"Can I see that paper?" I asked of him.

Dad handed it to me. He drank coffee while he watched me read the article. I read it once, and then I reread it. Using my cell phone, I did a quick web search. I smiled as I discovered what my father had wanted me to find. Victorious, I held my cell phone to him.

After seeing my results, he laughed and then clapped. Rafy and Mom were suddenly curious as to what my phone said.

"Wenceslao Santiago Vizcarrondo - the reporter - is the second cousin to the Santiago cousins - the boys whose father was killed in the diving accident," I proudly said.

Rafy took my phone and read the obituary for José Santiago Gonzalez - the victim who'd left behind three grieving sons and a newly-wealthy widow.

"What's the lesson here?" I asked my father.

"There are two lessons here," he said as he set his cup down. "First: always question a person who seems to be too curious about events that are unrelated to them. Second: family never forgets."

Impressed, I stared at my brilliant father. Before retiring, he'd been a full-time insurance investigator. Before that, he'd been an insurance salesman. In my youth, I'd learned many a lesson from him while I'd accompanied him on his insurance claim investigations. He wasn't done teaching me.

I let out a breath. "Not much gets passed you, Dad."

He smiled at me and patted my hand. "No. And nothing gets passed you," he asserted.

I beamed, feeling happy that I was still able to make my Dad proud.

"Great. Ignore your son, the detective," Rafy whined.

"You are great at what you do, *Hijo*," Dad said. "You are better than most at picking out spoken lies. You are great at cultivating informants. That is far more valuable than researching newspaper articles."

"Thanks, Papi," Rafy said.

A quarter of an hour later held me placing my suitcase in the trunk of my Dad's sedan. I took the time to stare at my parents. They looked older than when I'd seen them last. I was missing a lot by being so far away.

"Twenty-seven degrees and raining," Rafy said as he glanced at his cell phone.

"Do you mean Celsius? Cause it's pretty warm here today."

Rafy laughed out loud. "Celsius? I am talking about the temperature in Chicago! Fucking cold, Marta - and wet."

I groaned. Rafy fiddled with his phone and then laughed again. "Huh. How about that? It's 80 degrees Fahrenheit here, which in Celsius is 27 degrees. I don't know if that is ironic or unfortunate. Probably ironic for me, but unfortunate for you."

I wouldn't let him bait me - not so soon before I was to leave. "Do you think that you would ever want more than the Arecibo Police Department? Job-wise?"

Rafy closed his phone and looked at me. "Sometimes," he whispered. "But I got a good thing going over here. I don't take that for granted."

"It's not wrong to want more."

"I got a lot," he said as he shrugged. "A hot wife, my parents, twin boys, and the admiration and fear of my fellow police departments. And I'm living in paradise. It's plenty."

"Then I'm glad," I said.

After hugging him goodbye and sending my love to Wanda and the boys, I got in the backseat of my Dad's car. I let out a breath as we drove away from my childhood home. Thinking quickly, I sent a text to Rafy. He answered. "*Yes, it is still hard to leave Mom and Dad's house - and I live right down the road.*"

I couldn't tell if his response hurt or helped me. Still, I held our shared feelings as comfort while my parents drove me further away from Arecibo and closer to the airport. The goodbye was sad, as it always was. Mom cried. Dad was stoic. I cried, but I didn't sob. I was sure to hug them long.

"Keep an eye out on Hector for me?" I asked.

Mom smiled. "Of course. I am there every other day. Your brother is there a lot, too."

I let out a breath. "I will try to come back soon."

"I will pay for your ticket next time," Dad said.

I hugged my father again. I squeezed their hands before heading out to my gate. I could not find feelings of excitement as I sat on a seat outside my plane. Excitement could not be found onboard the flight, either.

I scrolled through pictures on my digital camera. It held beach images, party ones, picnic ones, and of pizza, rotisserie chicken, roasted pork, and deep-fried goodness.

My DNA was on the island, but my life wasn't there, I told myself.

"It's hard to leave," said the woman seated next to me.

I turned to face the woman seated in the middle seat of my row. She was an older woman of Hispanic descent and dressed very well.

"Were you there on vacation?"

She swallowed a few times. "I was there to spread my father's ashes. He kept saying that he would make it back there before he passed. He never did."

I felt tears fill my eyes. "Goodness. I am so sorry."

She sighed. "Yeah. Me too. But Dad had a very good life in the states. You can't tell by looking at me, but my mother's white. My parents were very happy," she said as she smiled.

"Is your mother still around?"

She smiled and nodded. "Yes, but she's in a nursing home - Alzheimer's. She keeps calling for my Dad, but she smiles and laughs all the time. Thank God for that. My younger brother is there now, keeping her company. Between him and I, we gave our parents seven grand-children. They were proud."

"That's good to hear."

"Are you leaving someone on the island?"

I thought of telling her about my son but held that back. "My parents. My brother and my nephews. But, I am going back to Chicago and the life I built there. Not the easiest thing to do in early December."

She laughed out loud. "Preach. I live in Milwaukee, myself. Cold as hell there, but it's home." She took the time to look out the window. "This island is a dream: a paradise, kind of. I can come here from time to time. I can have good times and remember old ones. My Dad's home now. I can visit him here."

30

I sighed. "That's sad. If someone on the plane starts singing 'En Mi Viejo San Juan,' I am going to throw myself onto the hot tarmac."

My seat neighbor laughed out loud. "That's depressing and hilarious." She let out a breath. "It is nice talking to you, but I am too sad to talk. If you don't mind, I am going to listen to some music and read a book."

"It was nice talking to you, too. Enjoy your music."

She gave me a half-smile before putting her earbuds in. I closed my eyes and forced myself to think of things besides my aging parents, my laughing brother, my growing nephews, and my son buried outside of the cathedral where my parents had been married.

Three and a half hours later held me putting on a heavy coat and removing my carry-on from the overhead compartment. I took a breath as I left the plane.

My phone rang just as soon as I turned it on. I laughed when I saw who was calling me.

"How was your flight?" asked Melissa.

"It was...a flight. Leaving the warm Caribbean and coming back to cold Chicago."

"Tell me about it! Brazil is beautiful! Our room - I mean - our *rooms* overlook the ocean!"

I noticed Melissa's slip but did not address it.

"Please tell me you are drinking colorful, fruity, boozy drinks," I begged.

She laughed out loud, sounding relieved. "Caipirinha!" she exclaimed. "It isn't colorful, but it is so good! And the weather! My goodness. But we'll be back in Chicago in two days! I can't wait to catch up with you!"

"Do you need to pick you up from the airport?" I asked.

"I don't think so, but I'll let you know by tomorrow. Niels might want to hire a car."

"But you cannot forget your female friends," I insisted. "Think about it."

She laughed. "I will. I have to go now, but I am so happy to hear that you made it back okay."

"Thanks! I'll wait to hear from you. Enjoy your last days there!"

"I will! ¡Adios!"

I smiled and disconnected. Seconds later, my phone rang again.

"Marta!" Jane Knight excitedly said.

I laughed. "This is her."

"I am so glad you are back. Look, I am going to need you here tomorrow morning EARLY. Tim and I threw a HUGE party last night, and the place is a mess."

"Lovely," I said on a sigh.

"Hey. None of that. That's why I pay you the big bucks."

"I will gladly be there tomorrow morning."

"How was your vacation?"

"Nice. Warm. Fattening."

"As all good vacations should be. But I have to go now. I will see you tomorrow morning."

"I'll be there."

I made it to baggage claim. I missed my Mom and my Dad, and I almost missed my brother. While I wasn't looking forward to my quiet, empty apartment, I couldn't wait to get back to my comfortable bed. I looked forward to seeing Melissa, Jane, and even Doña Justa - my landlady.

Doña Justa would ask lots of questions about my vacation. I would answer them as well as delivering the Puerto Rican treats she'd requested.

Once I retrieved my suitcase, I nervously headed to the curb outside of baggage claim, where I would await my ride.

I was glad that I'd taken the time to reapply my makeup and comb my hair. I almost wished I had a beer because I needed something to calm my nerves.

I still couldn't believe that I'd called *him* for a ride - the detective that occupied my thoughts. Why had I called *him*? What had I done?

Standing in the cold, I had time to dwell on my stupid life choices - mainly because I'd called him. More so, because he was not yet there.

What in the hell had I been thinking? Why did I ask him to pick me up from the airport? Airport pickups are strangely vulnerable occasions. You go from one place far from home and come back with your belongings while waiting for a caring face to take you back to what was familiar.

But what did I do? I asked a cute cop for a ride. I could have kicked myself. Why didn't I ask him out for coffee? Or to meet him for a drink somewhere? Why did I put so much pressure on him by asking him to pick me up at the airport?

A cold breeze had me set my purse on my suitcase while I pulled my jacket collar up. The frigid blast passed but left me with a feeling of unease. Had it been an omen?

Hands crazy cold, I pulled my cell phone from my pocket and looked at it. I'd been waiting outside for ten minutes.

Why would a police officer be late? Who would get in the way of a cop in a marked vehicle? Had something happened to him?

Alarmed, I called his cell phone. It went straight to voicemail. I let out a breath and spoke.

"This is Marta. I'm at the airport. You aren't here yet. I'm hoping that you are okay and not injured. If you are okay and aren't making it, well, I wish you would have texted me or something." I let out a breath and looked down the street once more. "I think I'm going to make my way home on my own. I have stuff that needs refrigerated ASAP. Goodbye."

I hung up and dropped the phone in my pocket. Forlornly, I made my way to the taxi line. The driver smiled at me as I approached him, and I mirrored the gesture, as it might the only 'welcome back' I would get.

Chapter Five

A musty smell is not something anyone wants to come home to. It was why I availed my clients with the option of having me come to their homes while they were on vacation. I'd water their plants, open a window for a bit, and would take care of their mail. Pet services were an add-on that they took advantage of, too.

I did not own a pet, as I did not want the maintenance that came with them. Or maybe it was the commitment I was afraid of. Perhaps it was the fear of having to be there for something or someone. I was used to being on my own. While I was always ready to lend a hand, I was scared to ask for one.

Doña Justa - my landlady - wasn't home. I would deliver the *pasteles* to her middle-level-apartment later that evening. After huffing it up the stairs to my second-level apartment, I left my carry-on and my purse in the living room. I wheeled my suitcase to the kitchen. With a grunt, I heaved it onto my kitchen table. I removed the frozen foods from it and set them in the freezer. The beer I placed in the fridge.

I noticed something in the freezer I'd forgotten about. I pulled the New York-Style cheesecake out and served a slice for myself.

I moaned in pleasure as I chewed the divine goodness. The crunch of the graham-cracker crust coupled with the sweet, cool, and soft texture of the cake paused my feelings of rejection and loneliness. I had another bite.

I could appreciate how folks got overweight. Food was a perfect vehicle to the land of distraction. While I enjoyed the ride and the destination, I had the restraint to hit the brakes.

My phone rang from my coat pocket.

"How did you make it in?" asked Melissa.

I laughed. "Alive and cold, but here."

"Did you get a ride?"

"From the most polite of taxi drivers."

"Okay. I am glad to hear it. I have to go now, but I'll see you soon."

"That's great! Did you get a tan?"

"You know I did!" she said as she laughed.

Curious, I asked a risqué question. "Meet any cute Brazilian men?"

She was quiet for a moment, which was telling. Quickly, I supplied an out for her. "I'd have a hell of a time understand Portuguese. I can make out Italian and some French. But Portuguese? So hard!"

"Yes!" she echoed. "So hard to speak, but so easy to admire," she said she laughed. "No - I didn't meet any cute Brazilian men. I was too busy working."

"I hear that Argentinian men are gorgeous," I added.

"They are! The most gorgeous male models are from Argentina!"

I was going to say something else, but she grew quiet. "Look. I have to go now, but I am looking forward to catching up!"

"Yes. I'll be by the firm tomorrow to air it out."

"Thank you!"

"Sure thing! Have a great last night there."

"I will."

With that, Melissa disconnected. Almost immediately, my phone rang again. I looked at the number but didn't recognize it, save for the Puerto Rican code.

"Hello?"

"*Hola Marta! Te habla Elena Matos.*"

"Hi, Doña Matos. What can I do for you?"

"I didn't know you were leaving today! I thought it was tomorrow."

I rolled my eyes, as I knew that I'd been clear about my departure date. "I apologize for the confusion."

"Of course, of course. Look; I want to hire you."

I leaned back in my seat. "I don't know how that is possible anymore, Doña Elena. Not that I don't want the work. It's that I only accept cash payments."

"Will you make an exception?"

I shook my head. "No. My terms are strict."

She let out a breath. "I will make a special trip to Chicago to get you the cash."

That surprised me. "That sounds like a lot of trouble. Are you sure it's worth it?"

"It is," she asserted.

I shrugged. "Well. Okay. That works."

"I will call you when I arrive."

"Okay. I will wait for your call."

She disconnected without saying goodbye. I stared at the phone while questions flooded my brain. I left my half-eaten slice of cheesecake on the kitchen table and made my way to the dining room. Once there, I grabbed a yellow steno pad and a pen. I began to write questions down.

- *Why does Elena want to find this person so badly?*
- *Why would she drop four-hundred dollars on a ticket just to pay me a five-hundred-dollar deposit?*
- *Even if she has a lot of cash, why go through the trouble of hiring me? Why not hire someone else?*

I wrote down what I knew in a separate section.

- *Doña Elena Matos Boria wants to find her great-aunt's granddaughter - her second cousin. She believes it is this girl.*
- *Doña Elena has a lot of cash and is bored; that's how she can afford to drop some money on a ticket to Chicago. Perhaps she is reliant on my connections to find this person.*

- *Perhaps there is more she isn't telling me.*

I considered my last sentence a bit. Doña Elena was not telling me everything. But did that matter? I was not owed her trust. I was owed money for the labor I would undertake for her.

My other phone rang - my non-sleuthing phone. I had a sinking suspicion as to who might be calling.

"Hi Marta," said Detective Connelly.

I let out a breath. "Hello, Kevin. How are you?"

"Look...I want to apologize for not picking you up at the airport."

"Did something happen to you? Are you well?"

He groaned. "No. I'm fine. Uninjured."

"Ummm...why couldn't you pick me up?"

"Something came up. Didn't the cabbie tell you? I hired a cab for you. He was supposed to relay the message."

Anger filled me. "You ordered a cab for me?"

"Wait. Didn't you take it? How'd you get home?"

"That's not your concern, Detective Connelly. I got myself home, like the grown woman I am."

He moaned. "I'm sorry that I wasn't there."

"It's not your problem, Detective."

"Please call me Kevin."

"I will *not*," I snapped. Forcing myself to be calm, I spoke again. "Don't worry yourself, Detective Connelly."

"I would like to explain myself."

"There's no reason to do so."

"Stop being so cold!"

"Fine!" I railed. "You could have texted me! You could have called me! But you didn't. I think that you failed to do those things because you changed your mind at the last minute. Which is your prerogative," I said as I let out a breath. I needed to keep my cool. I didn't want to give the detective more of myself than he merited.

"Can I come over?"

"Hell no. There's no reason for you to come over. And I have to go now."

"Marta, I'm sorry."

I shrugged. "That's fine. Goodbye now."

I hung up on him. The phone rang again. It was him. I rejected the call.

It was a bullet dodged, his not coming to pick me up. Because he didn't want to. And who wanted to be rejected? Not me. So, it was done. I tried. It didn't work out. It wasn't meant to be. I was fine.

I repeated the platitudes for the rest of the evening.

Chapter Six

Jane Knight, Esquire, was behaving oddly.

"I am so sorry that things are so untidy!" she said as she greeted me at the door.

I looked around at the dining area off her kitchen. While there were a few stray cups and plates, it didn't look that bad.

"It's fine," I said. "How are you?"

She beamed. "I am good. I am well," she added.

I stared at her, and she stared back.

"Goodness! I don't have makeup on! How could I have forgotten to put that on?"

I could feel my head tilting a bit. It was true; Jane had no makeup on, which was odd. She made it a point to get ready early in the morning, every morning.

Just then, Tim - her husband and an attorney - walked in the kitchen, wearing nothing but a robe and a smile.

"Hello, Marta! How was Puerto Rico?"

I forced my grimace into a smile. "It was good—great food, fun times, and family. But life is here. In the cold and the slush."

Jane laughed. "Agreed! We are happy to have you back, though.

Tim came to Jane's side and rubbed her back. She looked up at him, and they shared a smile.

"Well, we'll leave you to it," Jane said. "You know where to find me if you need anything."

"Likewise."

I stared at the hallway even after they'd disappeared into it. Something was going on, and it was weird. Before I'd left on vacation, Tim and Jane's marriage had been very rocky. Something changed, as they seemed so close, which was good, of course. But weird.

"Whatever," I muttered before carrying on with my cleaning. Three hours later held me at Jamie's Pawnshop. Jamie's greeting was warm.

"Now, why would you come back here?" Jamie asked of me.

I laughed and then sighed. "Well...the food and the weather weren't the draw."

"Preach."

I didn't know how much to share with Jamie, as he'd only recently become friendly with me. I decided to put myself out there.

"Fun and family are there, but work and my future are here."

Jamie nodded and said nothing for a few seconds. "Sounds like my parents. They left Athens back in the fifties. In the beginning, they hated it. They hated it even more when I was drafted and went to Vietnam."

I had not known that about Jamie. I stopped sweeping and looked at him.

"How was that?" I asked.

"I made it back. My cousin did not."

I nodded. "My son didn't make it back from Iraq."

Jamie's eyes widened. He then took a breath and nodded. "I am sorry, Marta. I didn't know that."

I let out a breath. "It's okay. I'm not digging for sympathy. Just saying that I understand. Also, I like talking about Hector. He was a living, breathing person. Not a perfect man. When I talk about him, he's alive again."

"Hector's a great name."

"Thank you," I said as I smiled.

"My cousin Alexander was a bit of klepto. Loved watching pornos, too."

I laughed out loud, and Jamie did, too.

"It's nice visiting with those who aren't with us anymore," I said.

"Amen," he said.

"Well, let me get back to these floors."

Jamie nodded. "Sure. You can clean while we both fantasize about warmer climes."

"Amen to that."

Leaving the pawnshop, I felt a bit lighter. Jamie's goodbye had been friendly, which was warm on such a cold day.

My next stop was Erickson Ventures Chicago - Melissa Bollinger's place of work. Upon arriving, I noted that Niels and Melissa had not yet returned. I dusted, cleaned, and aired out the offices before setting small, potted plants on both their desks. Hopefully, the plants would clean the air a bit and would be a friendly welcome to the office's tenants.

My last cleanings for the day were for residential customers. The family members were present for the first cleaning; I did my best to ignore them while I tidied up. The inhabitants of the second home were absent, thankfully. I was able to relax while I made quick work of the house.

Driving home, I thought about what I'd achieved that day. I found that I enjoyed cleaning for my business-owner clients more than the residential ones. Jamie, Melissa, and Niels viewed me as a fellow professional and treated me as such. My residential clients considered me to be a bit more intrusive, which I could understand. I was seeing their private business; condom boxes and wine bottles in the trash. I saw their prescriptions, magazine subscriptions, refrigerator notes, and take-out food. I saw who regarded them warmly by looking at the Christmas cards on their mantels.

What were my residential customers seeing about me? What was I revealing? Next to nothing. I wore a brown uniform. My hair was tightly tucked into a bun. I said as little as possible. Except for Jane Knight - my sometimes attorney - I was a closed book. I looked at their stuff, judged them, and then took their money from them. Was it a fair exchange? Maybe not. But I did make it a point to clean the crap out of their homes. I also made it a point to charge a bit more than my fellow maids. It reminded them that I was a quality cleaner, and it helped insulate my bank account.

I didn't forget that I was replaceable. But my residential clients were replaceable, too.

Coming home, I couldn't stop the groan that escaped my lips just as soon as I saw the steps leading to my apartment. My week-and-a-half vacation of sitting in the sun and stuffing my face had gotten me out of shape, just a touch. Still, I trudged up the steps.

I groaned again when I saw the small, white paper rectangle wedged between my door and the jamb. Sighing, I removed it and read the front and the back.

"Call me," Detective Kevin Connelly had written on the back.

"I will *not*," I said as I crumbed the card.

Chapter Seven

It was not 100% sure that the ringing of my phone could be attributed to one person, but it sure as heck seemed that way.

I'd been back in Chicago for three days and three nights, and I was getting my groove back. Well, my cleaning groove, at least. My personal life groove was still in the crapper. Maybe if I picked up the phone, I could do something about my personal life woes.

I could not take the detective's calls, though, as there was the matter of my pride. Detective Connelly said that he would pick me up and the airport, and then he didn't. He deserved punishment for that. Did he deserve the right to give me an explanation? Maybe.

If I were a better person, I would probably give him a chance. I'd take the call and would let him talk. But I wasn't feeling up to being the better person.

Still, I stared at my ringing phone. Why shouldn't I take Kevin's call? Why was I acting like a twenty-year-old who had five other suitors pounding on her door?

The answer was pride: that, and time - I did not have it to waste.

I wasn't picky, either. I didn't need a 'clean slate' sort of man who didn't have a history, but I needed someone who knew what they wanted. I wanted a man could admit what he had time for and what he did not.

Detective Connelly had the luxury of time. He was handsome, a lawman, and still in his mid-thirties. He had the time to mess around and be picky. I was a touch jealous over it, which was probably why I was avoiding his calls.

I couldn't dodge his calls forever, though, as he had a history of making himself heard. I let out a breath and went back to watching my television, as I had a week-and-a-half's worth of shows to catch up on. I watched a Judge Judy episode, as I was starving for gossip. I usually got my gabbing fix with the exchanges I had with Melissa. However, she'd been making herself scarce. I'd got to Erickson Ventures at different times of day, too, just to try to catch her. Niels and herself were staying scarce, though. I took it as confirmation that their professional relationship had evolved into a personal one.

"Not my business," I said as I let out a breath and sunk even further into my couch.

Judge Judy was laying into a gold-digging divorcee when I heard a knock at my front door.

"What the hell?" I muttered.

Wearing a flannel nightgown and pants, I got off my couch and went to my peephole. Through the aperture, I saw a familiar red head of hair. I groaned and opened my door.

"Marta," Detective Connelly said as he gave me a once-over.

"Detective Connelly," I said, hanging onto the door and not admitting him to my apartment.

"Why are we back to that?" he asked as he let out a breath.

Crap. How maturely was I supposed to behave? I stifled a groan and opened the door, letting him inside my home.

The detective looked surprised as he walked in. With his hands in his pockets, he pivoted left and right, probably taking in my dining room, living room, and my kitchen.

"To what do I owe this pleasure?" I asked as I closed my front door.

"To the fact that you won't take my fucking calls," he angrily said.

"Don't cuss in my house."

He had the shame to blush. "Sorry. It's been a long day. Not an excuse, though. I know how you feel about profanity."

I shrugged. "I get it." Still, my arms were crossed over my chest.

"You're still mad at me," he said.

I let out a breath. "Would you like some coffee?"

He smiled. "Yes. Please."

Ten minutes later held us at my kitchen table.

"This is very good," he said as he sipped my coffee.

I decided not to be as mad. Detective Connelly was company, after all. And I had manners. Also, it was nice to talk to someone in person. And he was easy to look at.

"I'd accuse you of small-talking me, but I happen to know that this is pretty darned good Puerto Rican coffee."

He beamed. "It is."

I leaned back in my chair. "I'm punishing you. That's why I'm not taking your calls."

His smile fell. He set his cup back on its saucer before speaking again. "I get why. I wish you'd stop being mad, though."

"I put myself out there when I asked you to pick me up. You didn't come."

"I ordered a cab-"

I stopped him with a hand. "I'm not done talking."

He nodded, and I continued speaking.

"Call it my police background. The fact that I clean for people and the fact that I watch them. I put a lot of stock into non-verbal communication. You didn't pick me up. I took that as a signal that I was asking too much of you. Was I wrong?"

Kevin swallowed and looked away. I was stunned to see that his eyes were shiny. When he turned to look at me again, his eyes were clear.

"At the time, it didn't seem like a big ask. I was excited about seeing you again. But the day came, and I panicked. You are intimidating. Airports are fucking weird. I mean, I haven't seen you for two weeks, and I was supposed to pick you up and Uber you home? Then what? That wasn't a date. It was a favor."

I opened my mouth to speak, but he stopped me.

"I'm talking now. Fuck. If I could turn back time, I would have told you that if I picked you up, that would have had to have coffee with me. Maybe lunch. But I didn't. Perhaps I should have said no to picking you up and asked you for a date instead."

"Why couldn't you pick up the phone and tell me that? Why didn't you send me a text? Why did you think I'd be okay and not angry over you leaving me outside on a cold curb?" I angrily asked.

"Because," he angrily retorted. "Look at you! You are fucking gorgeous! In your frumpy nightgown and your gorgeous dark hair. You are smart, intimidating, and you scare me," he added.

I chuckled and then groaned. I rubbed my arms and looked around while I tried to find the courage to say what I wanted to.

"You're intimidating! You're a cop. Cute and redheaded. Young and funny. But I had to try. It fell flat, but I had to try-"

My speech ended just as soon as I felt Kevin's hand on my arm. He pulled me close, landing his mouth on mine. Shocked, I closed my eyes. Kevin's lips were soft as they pecked mine, time and again. I sighed. I might have even shuddered. It had been so long since I'd been kissed - and in so proficient a manner.

The astute detective got the signal. He got up from his seat and pulled me from mine so that he could deepen the kiss.

Damn. My coffee tasted good - especially on Kevin's tongue.

When Kevin's hands made it to my hips, I shoved him away. I took a breath and a step back.

"Wow," he said as he took a breath. "Jesus Christ."

"Profanity!" I admonished.

"Sorry," he apologized.

"Are you Catholic?"

He smiled. "Of course."

I rolled my eyes and shook my head. "I can't believe I asked that."

"That was an awesome kiss," Kevin said.

"You had no right to do that."

He shrugged. "I had to try. I had to try to make up some ground."

I became angry again. "No. You can't go from leaving me at the curb to kissing me at my apartment."

His face fell.

"How the heck did you make it to my apartment?"

He laughed. "I brought your landlady some donuts."

"Darn Doña Justa and her sweet tooth."

Detective Connelly laughed out loud. "I could get you some, too."

"Should I make a joke out of that?"

He groaned. "Please don't. You are a lot funnier than that."

I let out a breath. "You need to go."

"Okay," he answered, but did not make a move to leave. "How do I make things up to you?"

I shrugged. "I don't know."

"Give me something. Please," Kevin begged.

I shook my head. "No. You figure something out on your own that doesn't consist of coming to my house at ten p.m. and kissing me while I am wearing a nightgown."

"That's kind of the ideal situation," he teased.

"Kevin!"

"Was kissing you going too far?"

I shrugged. "I don't know."

He beamed. "Then, I am going to get going while the getting is good."

I rolled my eyes and wondered if men ever reached an age where they were completely mature.

Kevin walked to the door that I opened but didn't walk through it.

"I want to hear about your vacation."

"You could have, had you picked me up."

"Crap. I still have to make up for that, huh?"

I shrugged. "You need to go."

"I love that you are so proper," he whispered.

Damn it. Kevin was making up ground. "Go. Good night."

"It is now," He said as he smiled.

I rolled my eyes and laughed as I gently pushed him out the door and locked it behind him. I heard him whistling as he walked down the stairs. I opened the door and stepped on the threshold.

"Stop whistling!" I stage-whispered. "You'll give my neighbors the wrong idea!"

He turned and beamed. "Yes, Ma'am."

I closed the door and locked it. And then I smiled.

"Damn him," I said as I sighed.

Chapter Eight

The best thing to do, I decided, was to act as if the kiss had not happened. I had to forget that Kevin kissed me in a way that knocked my socks off - that he'd kissed me in a way I hadn't been kissed in years. I had to ignore the fact that he'd awoken something in me that had been dormant for so long.

Encouragement would have been irresponsible and premature. Still, the intense effort of ignoring the kiss took a lot of work, and focus, too. So much so, that I nearly jumped a foot in height when I felt a strange hand on my shoulder.

"¡Amiga! It's just me!" said Melissa Bollinger.

I sat back on the women's bathroom floor of Erickson Ventures Chicago.

"You scared me," I said as I turned to face my friend.

"I didn't mean to," the pretty blond said. "Man. What was I thinking? You are a maid, and you are cleaning, and who knows how many times folks have tried to assault you, and here I am touching your arm when you are so clearly focused on the task at hand, and I'm so sorry!"

I laughed out loud. "It's okay. There's no need to dig that deep. I was lost in thought. Honest to God. I am having zero assault flashbacks. I promise."

She let out a breath and sat down on the bench by the sinks. "Whew! Thank God."

I stood up and laughed as I saw her footwear. "My goodness! Those pink pumps are to die for!"

Melissa laughed and moved her ankles around, showcasing her shoes. "Aren't they? I got them in Brazil! Look," she said as she stood up. "I can wear this camel-colored suit and still look professional, but with these heels, I still look fun!"

"Yes. You pull that off well!"

She laughed. "I'm hugging you now. I haven't seen you in two weeks!"

I smiled and hugged her back before releasing her. "So, Brazil was good?"

She sighed and sat down again. "Well, the business part was hectic. Some folks don't like taking advice," she said as her eyebrows lifted, "even when it comes from an experienced, educated standpoint. Even when they are paying top dollar for it!"

"Sounds frustrating."

"It is. But what can you do?"

"Not much. How was the personal stuff?"

I noticed her pinched lips and rapid eye blinking before she gave me a big smile. "It was fun. Niels and I worked a lot. Still, I made it a point to go out and eat and shop."

"Obviously," I said. "Would you like to hear about my Puerto Rico vacation?"

44

"Yes!" she exclaimed. "But not now. I have a call to make. But drinks! We should get drinks tonight!"

"I would love that."

"I'll text you with details later."

"I'm glad you're back."

"I'm glad you're back!" she whispered before going back to her office.

As promised, Melissa texted me to meet for drinks at a place near her condo. I was familiar with the area, as I'd helped her with a stalker problem just a few months passed. Thankfully, that was in the past.

At the bar, she greeted me with a hug. "I didn't think to ask you somewhere closer to your place," she said as she escorted me to a small table by the bar.

I shrugged. "This is good, and a welcome change of view," I said as I looked around.

It was a dark bar that was kind of swanky, but not so much that it was uncomfortable. The décor was fancy, but not overly much. The good-sized crowd consisted of professionals still wearing their business suits. I wore dark jeans, black boots, and a leather jacket.

"I love this look," Melissa said as she waved at my jacket.

I laughed. "Put any black rags together, and they look good."

"There was some thought to this assembly," she said.

I laughed. "Okay. Maybe a little bit."

"And me in my office duds," she said as she rolled her eyes.

"You fit in better with this crowd. They are still dressed from work, too."

"Which isn't good," she earnestly said. "Sure, the threads are pricey, but where's the effort?" she asked of me. "Life isn't just about work, but we act as if it is," she said on a sigh.

Something was weighing on her mind and her heart, I knew. Still, I wouldn't poke. Not until she volunteered something.

"It sounds like you require a non-work vacation. A recharge!"

She nodded. "I do. Next time you go to Puerto Rico, I am going with you."

I laughed out loud. "That's fine by me. How about a trip before then, though? Maybe Miami or Pennsylvania?"

She sighed. "My dad's folks are from Hanover, P.A."

"I've never heard of it."

"That's okay. It's not exactly a vacation mecca."

I nodded and then accepted the drink that the bartender had given me.

"A Brazilian drink," Melissa said with a smile.

I smiled before having a sip. "Very good. I can see what you mean about the color, though."

"Drinks should be colorful and fruity, I think. This drink isn't that."

"Yes, but Brazil isn't in the Caribbean. Maybe they aren't as colorful there."

"Great point!" Melissa said. "Maybe there's something to that."

I stared at her a bit. I wanted to steer the conversation back to vacations. "So, maybe that part of Pennsylvania isn't like Miami or Cuba or even Brazil. But, getting away helps with perspective."

"Did you come back with that? Perspective?"

I let out a breath as I considered it. "I came back with a greater appreciation for my parents. If I am honest, I came back feeling sad at being apart from them. Time is passing by so quickly. My parents are aging. I enjoy Puerto Rico as a vacation destination, but I live *here*. But I don't have much here, save for how I make a living. I think that's pushed me to work on developing a better personal life."

Melissa stared at me for a few seconds. She appeared to be a bit nervous.

"Are you okay?"

She laughed and shook her head. "Yes. Of course."

I wondered if she was going to tell me that she was sleeping with her boss. It occurred to me that no one else in her life knew about her affair.

"What about your personal life? What are you going to do about that?" I asked.

I hoped that I didn't come off too obtrusively.

"I need to work on building that. Something real, too. Something tenable and long term," Melissa said on a sigh.

I figured that was as much as she was going to tell me about her personal life.

"Vacation! I still think you should go on one - to Pennsylvania or Miami. It doesn't have to be a great, festive thing. Maybe just a weekend, even."

She stared at me as if her life depended on it.

"What do you think?" I prodded.

"This is what I think," she said.

She pulled her cell phone from her bag and mashed some buttons.

"What are you doing?"

"Booking a ticket."

I clapped. "Yay! Where to?"

"Pennsylvania. See my parents and my grandparents."

"How awesome!"

"It'll only be for three days, but that's something."

"It is," I insisted. "It's enough time for a few family meals, some time in the country, and away from Chicago."

"It is," she agreed.

Feeling proud of her and myself, I ordered another round of drinks.

"Will you be able to drive home?" Melissa inquired.

I laughed. "Well...confession time. I like rum. I like shots of rum. I indulge in them whenever I've had a rough day. When you have a few rough days in a row, you develop a tolerance. Not that I'm proud of it."

"I get it. What other secrets do you have to share?"

I let out a breath and considered it. "I don't think I can live in Chicago forever."

"I don't either," she said as she nodded. "But what does that mean for you? Puerto Rico?"

Tears filled my eyes, surprising me. "No. I need something bigger. That's kind of sad to me - admitting that out loud."

"I understand."

Our meetup came to an end too soon. I looked at my watch, and Melissa looked at her cell phone.

"Goodness. Where does the time go?" she asked.

"Agreed."

"We have to do this again. Next week!" my friend said.

I laughed out loud. "That works for me."

After a hug outside the bar, I headed for my vehicle and drove home. After parking outside of my apartment, I glanced at my cell phone, which had been on silent—no missing calls.

"Damn," I quietly cussed.

My pissy mode carried on to the next morning, unfortunately. How could I not be angry? Kevin kissed me and then left? What was he trying to do to me?

I used my anger and scoured Jane Knight's shower walls. Surprising me, she walked into the bathroom.

"Hello, Marta," she said.

"Hello, Jane," I said.

She smiled before going to her medicine cabinet. She seemed bubbly, which was not like her. I shook my head and went back to my cleaning.

"What's wrong, Marta?"

I mentally used a cuss word. I did not want to confide in Jane Knight. But then I remembered that she didn't have many friends. She'd never said as much, but I could tell.

"Man trouble, Jane," I said as I sighed.

She laughed out loud and then leaned on the wall by her sink. "No kidding?"

I nodded. "Yeah. There's not much to tell. I am getting mixed signals, and I don't have time for that. I am forty. This guy is younger - 35 years old. He has time to mess around, as there are plenty of girls who will play that game. But I don't want to, and I need to figure out how to get out of it before it's too late, and I am in too deep."

Jane had gotten oddly quiet. I turned to face her and saw that she was crying. Shocked, I dropped my scrubbing pad.

"Jane? Are you okay?"

She shook herself and then wiped her face. "Shit. Yes. Of course. It's the fumes coming off the stuff you are using."

I nodded. "Of course. Yes. How about I put the fan on and close the door?" I said, tripping over myself to protect the vulnerable moment that Jane had dropped at my feet. "That way, you won't smell them as much. Also, I'm almost done here."

"Yes, that will work," she said. "You are doing good work here."

With that, Jane left. I stared at the closed door while I wondered what I'd said that elicited such a response. It could not have been the vinegar/dishwashing liquid/baking soda paste I'd made.

The bathroom had been my last space to clean for the day. I wondered what kind of mood I'd catch Jane in.

I needn't have worried, as Jane had left the condo. Tim was nowhere to be seen, either. I let out a sigh and shook my head.

"We women are mysteries, I guess," I whispered.

I gathered my things and carried on with my day.

Chapter Nine

Exchanges with women of mystery were the theme of the day. I'd just left Jamie's Pawnshop and was en route to a residential cleaning when my sleuth phone rang.

"Yikes," I said.

I thought about letting it go to voicemail but changed my mind. I had to make money that was independent of cleaning. I hit the speakerphone button and kept driving.

"This is Marta," I said.

"Marta? This is Doña Elena Matos Boria."

I nodded. "Hello. How are you?"

"I am in Chicago. By the Bean. When can you meet me?"

Surprised, I blinked a few times. "You mean you're here…in Chicago? Right now?"

"That's what I said," she drew out.

Doña Elena didn't sound too friendly at the moment. Maybe the cold was affecting her mood.

"How long are you planning to be in Chicago for?"

"Just today. I leave tonight."

"When did you get here?"

"This morning. When can you meet me?"

Wow. That was a lot of flying for one day. Doña Elena had my attention, admiration, and my bewilderment as well.

"I flew out here to pay you a lot of money," she said. "I don't want to have to wait any longer than I already have," she angrily said.

I stopped my car on the side of the road, where I tried to gather some patience.

"I appreciate your flying out here to deliver the funds, Doña Elena. I can certainly meet you today, but it must wait as I have a previous engagement that I cannot get out of."

"When can you meet me?" she impatiently asked.

I looked at my car radio for the time. "I can meet you in three and a half hours. At the Bean, if you'd like. But maybe not, as it is supposed to get very cold tonight."

"The Bean. Three and a half hours from now. I'll be there."

Doña Elena disconnected before I could get another word in. I stared at my silenced phone and wondered what my next move should be.

Doña Elena was not giving me the warm fuzzies anymore, and I was wondering if the gig would be as easy as I thought it would be. Thinking quickly, I reached into my purse for a notebook and a pen. I jotted down some notes.

- *Doña Elena purportedly flew out form Puerto Rico to Chicago to deliver me funds. She intends to leave the same day.*

- That much travel in one day indicates a lot of funds, also, desperation and impatience.
- She's not too nice anymore. Her dealings with me are wrought with anger and impatience.
- She seems to know a bit about Chicago. She had not indicated visiting Chicago before. She seems comfortable with the cold.

I added a note to myself.

- Who am I investigating?

With those heavy thoughts in mind, I put away my pad and rejoined traffic.

Three and a half hours later held me outside the Bean. It was cold, but thankfully, I'd dressed warmly.

Also dressed warmly was Doña Elena, who strode my way. I greeted her politely.

"Hello, Doña Elena."

"Hi. I have the cash deposit."

She reached for her purse - a Coach one - and retrieved a magazine for me.

"It's in there," she said.

I appreciated her discretion but still checked the envelope within the magazine to verify the money she'd given me.

"You are very determined to find your niece."

"I am," she said. "Can you do it?"

I shrugged. "I'll do my best, but I won't guarantee that I'll find your niece. I'll keep the deposit. You can get the rest of the cash to me as I get more information to you."

"I'll mail you a check."

I shook my head. "No. My terms are the same."

"You expect me to fly out here to pay you *again*?"

Looking at her, I made a quick study of Doña Elena. Her winter clothing fit her well. Her jacket was a Canada Goose one. Her pants and winter shoes did not look new, either.

"I am going to do my best to work within the deposit. But, should I need more time and money, you are going to have to come back out."

She grunted and rolled her eyes. "It's so cold out here."

"You are comfortable in the cold, Doña Elena. You'll be fine."

"You can tell that?" she asked as she squeezed the handles of her purse.

I nodded. "Yes, but that's not important. What is important is that I find your niece. I have what I need to get started. I will call you on Monday to let you know what I've gotten so far."

"Fine. You do that."

I let out a breath. "Well. Goodbye, then."

"Goodbye," she said. She then turned around and walked back the way she came.

I watched her for a couple of minutes before going back to my car. Doña Elena was an enigma. I needed to learn more about her. Lucky for her, I wouldn't count that against the deposit she'd paid me.

Once home, I had a shower and a quick dinner. After, I grabbed my phone and tried calling my dad. It went to voicemail. I called my mother but got the same result. Finally, I called my brother.

"*Aha. Aha. Dame un momento,*" he said in Spanish.

I groaned out loud.

"Hey. You chill. You're the one that called me," Rafy said.

"Why do your phone greetings suck so much?"

"Because it's my stupid little sister calling me."

"I'm not stupid!" I said, feeling like I was fourteen all over again.

"Calm down," he said. "I'm stepping outside the office right now."

"You working a late night?" I asked, instantly feeling guilt for jumping down his throat.

"Yeah. Getting ready for a movie that's going to film here in the pueblo."

"That sounds nice."

"Sounds nice," Rafy scoffed. "Let me tell you; this actor? The protagonist? A fucking prima donna."

I laughed. "What's the actor's name?"

"Can't tell you that. I signed a non-disclosure agreement."

"Ah, well. I understand."

"Why'd you call?"

I let out a breath. "Remember Doña Elena?"

"Yeah. What of her?"

So, I told him about her flying out to Chicago as well as her abrasive behavior. He was quiet for a bit.

"Did you try calling Dad?"

"Yeah. I couldn't get Dad or mom."

"Yeah. You don't want to share those details with Ma. She won't keep her yap shut about it."

"I know."

"They are at a wake for a family friend or something like that."

"Oh," I said. "I have a weird feeling about Elena. Like, in PR, she shows one face, but in Chicago, she shows another."

"That doesn't sound weird. The states are different. People adjust according to their surroundings."

I sighed. "I guess. I just think it's a good idea to know who I am getting into business with."

"Well, we know her pedigree—kind of. We know who her people are and who she married. Heck, we know who she buried. Some people are skilled at keeping secrets. Who knows what she's done or what she gets into?"

"Thanks for the clichés. I was hoping for something more tangible."

"I don't know what to tell you, Marta!" he impatiently said. "She seems like a bored, middle-aged woman who wants to pay you to find someone for her."

While I was grateful for my brother's time, I knew that my father would be the better person to bounce ideas off of. Dad was better at nuances while my brother was blunter.

"Look; I'll ask around. I think I know a guy who knew her husband pretty well."

"Why not her second or third husband?"

"She would have been more vulnerable with her first husband. She would have revealed more stuff."

"Good point."

"Yeah, it's almost as if I do this shit for a living."

I let out a breath. "Thank you. I miss you guys."

His pissy tone disappeared. "We miss you, too," he gruffly said. "You know where to find us."

"I do."

"I gotta go back in. I'll call you if I find anything."

"Sounds good."

With that, I hung up the phone. Seconds later, it rang again. I let out a breath when I saw the number. I let it ring a couple of times before picking it up.

"Detective," I said.

He groaned. "Marta! Enough of that."

I let out a breath. "You aren't out of the woods yet."

"I'm downstairs, and I have donuts."

"You're here?!" I exclaimed.

"Yeah. Come down and open the gate."

"But...I'm wearing a nightgown."

"Put a coat on. And hurry up! I'm freezing my nuts off."

"Nice," I said as I hung up on him.

Quickly, I headed downstairs to admit him. Darn. Kevin looked so handsome. His red hair looked golden under the lamppost light, and his eyes seemed brilliantly blue.

"Can we go in?" he asked.

"Yeah."

He followed me up the stairs and into my apartment. I closed and locked my front door. When I turned around, it was to find him crowding my space.

"What?" I asked.

He shrugged. "I was hoping for a kiss?"

I shook my head. "No. You stole the last one. It was premature."

He frowned. "Fine."

"I'll get coffee and plates."

The detective smiled. "Okay."

Minutes later, I was moaning over the donuts.

"Good, aren't they?"

I nodded. "I have to ask. Who bakes these donuts?"

"Small mom-and-pop joint about ten minutes from here."

"What is the place called?"

"They only sell to cops and firefighters. It's a small side gig for them."

I pouted. "Fine."

He stared at me a bit. "What have you been up to?"

"Cleaning. Hanging out. This and that."

He nodded. "A buddy of mine saw you at a bar a few nights back."

I blinked a few times. "A buddy of yours?"

"Yes."

"You mean a fellow cop, right?"

"Yeah."

I stared at him. "Are you having me followed?"

He laughed and shook his head. "No. He was at a restaurant across the street from the bar where you were."

"Oh? And how did he know to look at me? To look for me?" I angrily asked. "How did he know to get back to you with that?"

"Fuck. Why do you have to sound like a cop?"

"Because I used to be one. Answer the question!"

"I didn't know you'd gone to the bar. I...was fishing," he meekly said.

"Why?"

"I wanted to make sure you were okay, so I asked a patrolman buddy of mine who works this beat to keep an eye on your car and your place. The patrolman said he saw you wearing dressy stuff."

I sighed as I stared at him. His concern was sweet, but I didn't approve of his methods.

"Yes. I was at a bar. I was meeting someone."

"Who?" he asked.

"Why do you want to know?"

"Because I like you, and I don't want you to date another guy."

That was more honesty than I expected. "I was meeting a friend - a female one. For drinks."

He nodded. "Did you have a good time?"

I smiled. "Yeah."

The detective kept staring at me.

"What's on your mind?" he asked.

"How do you mean?"

"You look unsettled."

I stared at him a bit. "I'm wondering what we are doing," I asked as I shrugged.

He nodded and sat forward in his seat. "I think I want to date you," he said.

Butterflies and nerves filled me. I nodded. "Okay."

He kept staring at me. "Where does James fit in all of this?"

I stared at him a bit. "James Kostas?"

"Yeah."

I shrugged. "I don't know. Nowhere, I guess."

Kevin kept staring at me.

"You know when folks date, they go to places together."

"Do they?" he asked as he sat back in his seat.

"Yeah. It's been a while since I last on a date. That's not true. It's been a couple of months," I said as I looked at the calendar hanging in the kitchen.

"Who'd you go out with?"

I shook my head. "I'm not going to tell you that."

"It was the interpreter, right?"

I must have blushed. Kevin smiled.

"How'd that go?" he asked.

"Not great. Do you know anything about bad dates?"

He laughed out loud. "A thing or two."

"So, are you going to ask me out on a date or something?"

He nodded. "Yeah. You want to get dinner tomorrow night?"

I swallowed and looked at my nails. "That's kind of short notice. I'll have to look at my schedule."

He shook his head. "I already saw your calendar. You're in the clear."

I laughed.

"Okay. You going to stand me up again?"

His face fell. "No."

I nodded. "Okay. I just want you to know that if you don't think that this is going anywhere, you can just let me know. We'll call it good and go our own way."

Kevin took a breath and leaned back. "Why are you planning for a negative outcome?"

"I'm smart, I guess. I haven't dated in forever. I don't want to get in too deep if it isn't going anywhere. I don't want to waste my time, and I don't want to get hurt."

"Who does?"

"Dating's scary," I whispered.

He nodded. "Yeah. It is. But if we don't try, we don't know."

I stared at him a bit longer. "Well. We should probably call it a night."

He stood up. "Okay. I'll pick you up at eight tomorrow."

"Okay."

I walked him to the door.

"Can I have a kiss?"

I laughed and shook my head. "No."

"Had to try," he said with a smile. "Lock up. I'll see you tomorrow."

"Okay. Good night."

I closed and locked the door. I stared at it until I heard Kevin's footsteps go down the stairs. After, I began to pace.

I was nervous, scared, and excited. I was invested in Kevin Connelly, and it scared me. I resisted the urge to have a shot of rum, but I had to do something with my energy.

I went to the kitchen, where I grabbed a scrubber from a cabinet. I doused my sink in dishwashing fluid and then began to scour away at everything in there.

"It'll be okay," I whispered to myself.

Unless it wouldn't be okay, and even if it weren't, I would have known I tried, and that mattered.

Chapter Ten

A visit to the overrated (in my opinion) Panera Bread was the priority destination the following day. I was to meet Ada Barros - my bookkeeper/financial advisor. My ex-husband Anibal Robles (a certified public accountant with his own accounting business), had overreached (again) and lent me, free-of-charge, the use of one of his associates.

I wasn't stupid. I knew that it was Anibal's way to keep me close. It was a way for him to tell our son that he was still looking for me.

Maybe it was a bad idea for me to use Ada Barros' services, but the truth was that I needed them. And they were free.

I sat down at Ada's favorite table and waited. I bit into the too-hard cookie and drank the okay coffee while I looked around. The place was clean enough. There were plenty of people eating and nursing drinks while they worked on tablets and laptops.

I wondered why they didn't work at the library or their homes. Why would they come to a place like this? It occurred to me that maybe they wanted to be around other people. Maybe they lived alone. Perhaps they didn't like their co-workers. Perhaps here, they could lift their eyes from their screens and glance at other people like them.

Waiting for Ada gave me the time to consider my living situation. I liked it, even though I was lonely. Relief came when I went to clean for folks. Amusement came when I sleuthed.

Fifteen minutes into my crappy coffee had me realizing that Ada wasn't showing up. Grimacing, I reached for my phone and called her.

"Crap, Marta," she said in apology. "Any chance you can come to the office?"

I groaned on the phone. "Why can't you come here?"

"My car's in the shop, and I forgot to text you. Crap. Look at the time; I forgot to pick up my car."

"Fine. Is Anibal's new wife on the premises?"

"No. Gretchen isn't here."

I thought about the drive and let out a breath. "Fine. I'll be there in thirty."

Thirty-five minutes later held me parking at my ex-husband's place of business. Anibal had given it some sort of generic financial name, which was a smart move. He'd always been smart, though.

Ever nervous, I got out of my car and headed to the office. As soon as I entered the office, Ada stepped out of a small room to greet me.

"Marta. In here."

I followed her into her office and sat across her desk while she typed away at her laptop.

"How was the coffee at Panera?" she asked with a half-smile.

"Great," I said, forcing excitement into my voice.

Her brown, spectacled eyes looked up at mine. "Really?"

"No. It was crap. Like always."

She smiled and went back to her screen. "How was the trip to P.R.?"

I stared at Ada, wondering how much she'd tell Anibal. Probably all of it, or maybe none of it. Still, I could share, as it was common knowledge anyway; we were both Puerto Rican, and she could probably ask around to get the information.

"Well, it was good. My brother's great. My nephews are growing up, and my parents are growing old. I saw some old friends and family members. I went to the beach and ate too much fried food. It was a good visit, though. Great memories for the memory bank."

Ada looked glassy-eyed. I decided to rattle her cage a bit.

"What's sad is that you don't know when you'll see people again. My uncles, aunts, and cousins? I might have said my last goodbye to them."

Ada swallowed and blinked a few times before reaching for her iced coffee.

"I need to make it over there soon," Ada said.

"Yeah. I said that a lot. It took a close call to get me out there, though."

"What close call?" She asked as she looked at me.

I shook my head. "Oh. Just a work slip-up. Nothing of importance. What was important was the visit."

She let out a breath. "Okay. Lay it on me. How much money have you made?"

I gave her the low-down.

"You are still in the black, and edging slightly towards green. But you are getting older, and your job isn't getting easier. You need to secure another source of income."

"I'm working on that," I said.

"Good. Let's set some financial goals for the month. I am going to text you some links on HUD loans."

"Whoa. Not this again." I said, suddenly scared. A few months ago, Ada had mentioned my purchasing a home. I blew the advice off and had every intention of doing so again.

"Equity. You can borrow against it, and it is good for tax deductions. If you are in a jam, you can rent out a room or the whole place."

"I guess that makes sense." And it did. I would have to think about it.

"Good," was her reply.

I scheduled to meet with her the following month. After, I got up and looked at the door leading to Anibal's office. Anibal's entrance was guarded by a secretary who was less than attractive, and I chuckled.

"What's funny?" Ada asked of me.

I shook my head. "Nothing. Thanks, Ada."

"Sure thing."

I walked to the desk belonging to my ex-husband's secretary. She stared at me before speaking.

"Can I help you?"

"Yes. I'd like to talk to Anibal."

She blinked a few times. "Do you have an appointment, Miss...?"

"Morales," I answered.

"I can put you on the books for an appointment. Mr. Robles is very busy."

I nodded. "I understand. I want you to check with Anibal right now, though. Tell him Marta's here."

She shook her head. "He's on an important call right now."

Ada's head popped out from her office. "Tina? Call Anibal. Now," she enunciated.

Tina let out a breath and picked up the handset before spinning in her chair. "I'm sorry, Mr. Robles. There's a woman here who wants to see you. She won't make an appointment, and Ada's going on about it. The woman's name is Marta Morales."

Seconds later, Anibal's door opened. My ex-husband looked good - tubby around the waist, but good. He looked from me to Tina.

"Tina? *Never* make Marta wait. *Ever.*"

"Um. Yes, Sir. Okay," Tina said as she looked away.

"Am I understood?"

I let out a breath, as I felt guilty over my power-play. "Your secretary wasn't rude, Anibal - just efficient."

Tina looked like she was about to cry. Her hands shook as she rearranged pens on her desk.

"Marta. Come in. Please," my ex-husband said.

I did. Anibal closed the door behind me, and I took the time to admire his space. On the walls were pictures of Puerto Rico - photos he'd taken. A large, poster-sized image of a teenaged Hector riding a bike stopped me in my tracks.

"Damn," I said.

Anibal nodded and swallowed.

"The pictures I have of him in my apartment? I have them memorized. But, when I go to a family member's house, and I see a picture of him that I'd forgotten or never seen before? It stops my heart," I said as I touched my chest. "I know he wasn't just mine," I said as I looked at Anibal. "He was your son and big brother to your other children; grandson to our parents and nephew and cousin to many."

Anibal pulled a tissue from a box on his desk.

"I'm okay," I said to him.

"I'm not," he said as he dabbed his eyes.

He gave me his back for a moment; I assumed that he was trying to compose himself. Then my own eyes filled with tears.

"Damn. Can I have a tissue?"

Without looking my way, he handed me the entire box. "Take them all," he said as he cleared his throat.

"Cool. Free financial advice *and* tissues. That's full service," I said as I smiled.

Anibal chuckled and turned to face me. "You are still funny."

I shrugged. "I try. I make myself laugh."

He cleared his throat and then leaned on his desk. "Sit down, please," he said as he pointed to a chair.

I did.

"What brings you to my office?"

I let out a breath. "Have you tried reaching out to Waleska? About Adan?"

He took a breath and shook his head. "I...tried about a year and a half ago? She wouldn't talk to me."

"Have you heard about Grandparents' Rights? It's a thing here in Chicago. I'm thinking of looking into it."

Anibal reached to the tissue box and took it from me. He pulled one out and dabbed his eyes. "Fuck. It looks like I'll need to hang onto these."

"I'm sorry, Anibal."

Anibal shook his head. "No, no," he asserted. "Never apologize about coming to my office to talk to me about our son. Ever."

I nodded. "Okay. Well...I'm thinking of approaching her again in person. In a friendly way, that is. Before I think of hiring a lawyer."

"If you need a lawyer, you call me. I will pay for it."

I half-smiled. "I have a lawyer. But thank you."

His desk phone rang. He pursed his lips and then looked away from it, ignoring the call.

"How was Puerto Rico?"

I smiled. "It was...like it always is. Good, warm, sunny, tasty, and familiar. Full of nosy family members and friends."

He smiled and nodded. "Yeah. I need to get out there again soon."

I nodded. "Yeah. Well. Don't let me take up more of your time."

Anibal shook his head. "No. I wasn't doing anything that couldn't wait. How's your brother?"

"Rafy's good. Still running his mouth and antagonizing folks. But, doing well in the police force and at home, too. His boys are great."

"Wanda good, too?"

For a moment, a memory flashed before me - Rafy, Anibal, Wanda, me and little Hector sitting on the porch. Hector was petting my brother's now-passed German Shepherd. I could see my son's chubby baby hands and almost smell his baby-powder-scented back. I would go back if I could, but maybe I wouldn't. My nephews would not be around. My son would not have married and had a son.

"Wanda's good," I finally said. "Working as a psychologist for the Department of Health. Happily managing the twins' schedules."

"How about your folks?"

"Getting older. How dare my parents do that?"

My ex-husband's smile dropped. "Life finds ways to keep being cruel, I guess."

Just then there was a knock at the door. Anibal let out a breath and opened the door.

"What, Tina?" he impatiently asked.

His secretary cleared her throat. "It's your wife - Gretchen - on the phone. She says it's important."

Anibal let out a breath and dashed to the phone. "What?" he asked. He was quiet for a moment. "Who the fuck called you? Huh? Who called you?" he growled.

I gathered my purse off a chair and walked to the door. "I'll go, Anibal. I don't want to make trouble for you."

He stared at me for a while. "Sure thing, Marta. You know where to find me."

I looked up at the poster of our son. I saw Anibal in his features. "Okay, Anibal. Take care."

I walked out of his office and watched as the secretary did her best not to look at me. I glanced at Ada in her office. Her eyes were wide as they regarded me.

"Way to go," I said to her.

"It's not like that," she quickly said.

"Not my business. I'll see you next month," I said as I walked out.

Before I could open my car door, Anibal had made his way to me.

"I'm sorry about that."

I shook my head. "Not my business, Anibal. I dropped by unannounced."

"I don't care. Seriously, though, if you get a hold of Waleska and she is receptive, please let me know. Help me see Adan?" he asked as his voice cracked. "I have three other children, but none of them will ever replace my boy. I want to see his son."

I swallowed at tears. "You'll be my first call, okay? If I have to call a lawyer, I'll let you know."

"Okay," he said as I opened my car door.

He watched me as I climbed in. "Marta?"

"Yeah, Anibal?"

"I'm sorry," he whispered.

I closed my eyes for a moment. I wasn't too sure what Anibal was apologizing for, and I didn't want to know. I nodded and opened them again.

"Take care, Anibal. Thanks for the financial advice."

I was going to tell him that Ada was the one that ratted me out, but I didn't. No way I needed that kind of drama in my life.

Chapter Eleven

I shelved the drama that had unfolded at Anibal's office and went home to get ready for my date with Detective Kevin Connelly. I had four hours until then, but it was good to be prepared.

I stood in front of my open closet and stared. I needed time to go through my wardrobe to review my outfits. I had to decide what kind of message my clothing would send. I had to do my hair, but only just so. I couldn't straighten entirely as it would look too different from my everyday hair. My cosmetic choices would involve a similar sort of balancing act. I would wear eyeliner and a bit of mascara, a touch of lipstick, but not a bright shade.

"Why are you such a nutcase?" I asked of myself.

I shook my head and closed the closet door. I decided to get ready for my date forty-five minutes before it and no sooner. With that in mind, I grabbed the file I made for Doña Elena and sat down at my dining room table.

"Where to start?" I thought aloud.

At the beginning, of course. I had to put myself in Doña Elena's shoes. Having already placed her deposit into my 'consultation services' bank account, I pulled out my check card. I grabbed my laptop and visited Doña Elena's preferred DNA testing website. I scrutinized the testing service by visiting every single page, reading disclaimers and FAQs, and read reviews on it. Satisfied, I ordered a DNA test for myself using a brand-new email account.

Satisfied with that process, I got up and paced my living room a bit. I glanced at the folder containing my statements and assessments about Doña Elena, and I began to think.

Doña Elena was trying to find a distantly-related niece. But why? Curiosity? Maybe. Money? She had enough of that, so perhaps not. But maybe so. Who knew how rich people obsessed with money? Did they worry about money more than less financially affluent people?

With that in mind, I picked up my phone. I went through my contacts, and I considered who might best answer the kind of questions I had. I contemplated calling my father but then discarded the thought. Melissa might have been an excellent second choice but decided that I didn't want to bother her with my questions. I could have called Rafy, but decided against it; I wanted to bother him with more serious inquiries.

I could have asked Detective Connelly, but he might ask questions I did not want to answer.

That left one person. I dialed the number and was nervous all over again.

"Marta?" asked Jane Knight.

"Hi, Jane. Are you busy?"

"No, of course not. Just watching TV with the hubs."

Jane Knight was watching TV. That was flipping weird. She never watched TV, as she was always hustling and working. I discarded those thoughts, as they did not apply to the reason why I'd called her.

"Are you okay, Marta?"

I shook my head. "Yes, Of course. I just wanted to ask you something really quick."

"I'm all ears."

Polite and weird. Whatever.

"Um...what's your opinion about wealthy folks? Do they worry about staying rich? Do they worry about their futures more than middle-class people?"

I heard nothing for a moment. Seconds later, I heard a door open and close. Mentally, I placed Jane in her home office.

"Why do you ask? Did you find a safe full of cash or something?"

She sounded skeptical and a bit salty - more like her old self.

"No. My financial situation has not improved in that sort of way. But I am dealing with someone whose motivations confuse me. She is very well off, but she's hired me to find someone for her."

"Ah. The sleuthing," Jane said. I could hear the smile in her voice.

"No," I countered. "No. That's not it. I'm...consulting."

Jane let out a breath. "My phone can't be hacked. You can tell me stuff."

"How's that possible?"

"Do you know how expensive I am?"

"I do."

"Then why are you wasting my time with stupid questions?"

That sounded more like the Jane Knight, and I was intimidated all over again.

"Yes. I am sleuthing for a sketchy client. She wants me to find someone for her - someone who, at the outset, cannot improve my client's situation in life. This investigation makes me question my client's motives. Is it about money? Do rich people care about money?"

"Hold on a second. Your questions are getting good," Jane said. I heard the sound of wood squeaking and pictured her seated behind her desk. "Okay. If she's the type of person who puts a lot of value into her social station, then yes - she'll always worry about money. She might have more than enough of it, but that won't stop her from worrying about making more and keeping it."

"That fits. My client is condescending and insists on being addressed respectfully."

"Then it's about money. Probably," Jane qualified. "Or, it might be about settling an old score."

"Goodness," I said as I groaned.

"Tell me more," Jane prompted.

"Weren't you watching TV with Tim?"

"Fuck that boring shit."

I laughed. "Okay. Well, I met my client in Puerto Rico. I insisted that she pay me in cash. She didn't see me before I left, so I thought the job was off. But then she flew out here for one day to deliver the cash in person."

"Marta?"

"Yeah."

"Be careful with this one."

"Shit," I said, allowing myself a momentary cuss word.

Jane disconnected shortly after, which I was alright with. Having found more nervous energy, I paced my living room anew. I wrung my hands while wondering if I should discharge Doña Elena as a client.

"Think, Marta," I said as I let out a breath.

I could do it, I decided. I could find out what Doña Elena wanted to know. Or, I could do as much work as the retainer allowed for, and then I could stop.

Sore feet made me sit down. Rubbing my feet, I was reminded that my aging body could not clean forever. I had to keep Doña Elena as a client.

Two hours later held four discarded outfits on my bed, my face entirely made up, and half of my hair straightened with the other half was still wavy. I was officially freaking out.

My doorbell rang, making my freak-out intensify.

"What in the hell?" I said out loud.

I dashed to the peephole in my front door, through which I saw a tall, redheaded police detective.

"What are you doing here?!"

Kevin made a show of looking at his watch. "Umm...we have a date."

"Yes, but you aren't due for another thirty minutes! Why are you so early?"

He regarded my door with a look of disbelief on his face. "Are you giving me a hard time for being *early*?"

"No! *No*," I insisted. "There's early - that's like five or ten minutes early, and then there's *stupid* early, which is anything over fifteen minutes. Guess which kind of early you are?!"

Kevin had the nerve to laugh. "Do you want me to leave?"

"I want you not to be this early."

"Well, what do you want me to do, Marta? You were pissed because I stood you up before, and now, you're mad because I am too early."

Damn his intelligent reasoning. "Fine. I'll open the door for you, but you can't look."

He beamed. "Are you naked?"

"No, you dirty boy!"

He laughed out loud. "Fine. I won't look."

"I mean, you can open your eyes, but only once I've led you to the couch, and you've heard my bedroom door close. Okay?"

"Okay," was his answer.

"You'd better keep your eyes closed!"

"I will! Can you open the door already?!"

Thankfully, he abided by my wishes. I placed my hand on his surprisingly thick forearm while I guided him to the couch.

"I can't decide if I'm turned on or terrified," he said.

I let out a breath. "How so?"

"Are you naked? Or do you have scales and warts all over your skin?"

I scoffed. "I'm not naked, and I don't look like a troll. Trust me; you've seen me at my worst."

Kevin leaned back on the couch and smiled while his eyes remained closed. "Yay. You can leave me here," he said as he waved a hand at me. "I've got some fantasizing to do."

"You are a dirty boy."

"You don't know the half of it."

I left Kevin to his fantasies. I closed the door to the bedroom and stared at my reflection in the mirror. I had work to do.

Quickly, I ran the straightening iron through the wavy side of my hair. From the bottom of my clothing pile, I grabbed black pants and a gray silk blouse. I went light with the makeup and comfortable with my shoes.

When I opened the bedroom door, it was to see the detective staring at me, and quite seriously. I blushed. He smiled and then stood up.

"I like this - waiting on your couch as you get ready."

I smiled. "Was that the plan?"

Kevin laughed out loud. "No, but it worked out. Come on," he said as he presented his arm to me. "I'm taking you and your sense of humor out on a date."

I laughed. "Good. My sense of humor will give you a good time."

"How about you? Will you give me a good time?"

I let out a breath as I grabbed my purse. "I hope you have better game than that, Detective."

He laughed. "I do. I can't wait to give you my best bar pick-up lines."

I laughed again.

That was how I spent most of my evening with him - laughing and smiling. He did the same. We'd had dinner at a small restaurant I'd not heard of. After, we went down the street to an Irish pub.

"What do you have in Puerto Rico?"

"As far as what?" I asked before having another sip of my drink.

"Pubs. Do you have them there?"

I shook my head. "No. I think that's only a UK thing, I think."

"Where do you drink?" he asked as he sat back a bench seat.

"Well, wherever we can. Whenever we can."

He smiled. "Okay. But is there a character to your bars? A flair?"

I nodded. "Yeah. Maybe there's a bit of Spanish flair to the bars, but not too much. Puerto Rico's been doing its own thing for a few hundred years. I think that most Puerto Ricans would consider an ideal drinking situation as doing it with loved ones. Perhaps over a meal? Laughing. No judgment and no worries. Maybe drinking alone in medicinal capacities only."

"How do you drink?" he asked before sipping his beer.

"Here, or in PR?"

"Both."

I nodded. "In Puerto Rico, I drink socially, and usually beer. Here at home, I drink medicinally. A shot of rum here or there, if my day's been rough. Or if I have to listen to my mom harangue me."

Kevin smiled, so I continued.

"If Mom's getting dramatic, I might have a couple of shots. If my day has been stressful - or good, I'll have a celebratory slice of cheesecake."

Kevin leaned back in his seat as he stared at me. I discreetly let out a slow breath as I gazed at him. His blue eyes were so mesmerizing. They looked like a calm ocean, but mysterious like a darkening sky, too.

"How was your vacation?"

I sighed. "Just lovely. But maybe I'm a bit more charitable because I've been away from it for a couple of days now."

"Was it rough?"

"Well, staying in my childhood bedroom, listening to old arguments, condescension about my chosen profession and my mother forgetting that I'm a grown woman made for rough parts. Seeing my son's tomb was sad and happy. Being around family, warm weather, eating the great food, and even going to mass was good."

He stared at me.

"How was your day, Kevin?"

He let out a breath and looked at his beer. He then turned around to find someone. When the waitress came to view, he lifted a finger. She nodded, which was when Kevin turned back to me.

"It was hard and sad, Marta. I don't want to talk about it."

"Do you...lock the hard stuff up? Inside of you?"

Kevin's face went serious, and he stared at me for a moment before nodding. "Yeah. I shouldn't, though. I've got years left on the job. Other stressors are coming, I'm sure."

"Do you need me to be a distraction?"

"You are a distraction."

Butterflies filled my belly. The waitress came with his beer.

"Do you want me to tell you about my clients?"

"I do," was his answer.

I told him about some of the people I cleaned for, but not Jane or Melissa, as I guarded them carefully. He enjoyed hearing about my other clients and of past experiences.

"Can I ask you something?" I inquired.

"Sure."

"Do you ever have the luxury to say no to a certain case or a certain suspect? If they are too dangerous to handle? Can you do that - professionally or personally?"

Kevin's eyes widened as he appeared to consider my question.

"Yes. I can always ask for help. Sometimes a fellow detective will partner up with me. It doesn't mean that I always ask for assistance, though. Personally speaking, I don't think that I can turn away a job or a bad situation. My work means illuminating the dark."

I considered that as I looked around.

"Why do you ask?"

"I have a client. She might be a bad egg. She hasn't given me any evidence to prove that, but I've got a feeling, you know?"

"Are you in danger?"

"No."

"Stick with it. Keep an eye out. If the situation gets worse, ask for help. Ask me."

"Okay."

I looked at my watch. It was late.

"Bedtime?" he asked of me.

I laughed. "Yeah. I have work tomorrow."

"Okay. Let me get you home."

A feeling of peace settled within me as the detective drove me home. Safety, too. Maybe not my heart, but my person. It was one of the perks of dating a cop, I imagined. Kevin walked me up the stairs, but I stopped him at the door.

"Can I come in for a nightcap?"

I shook my head and smiled. "No. I'm sorry. It's late. You need to go to bed. I do, too."

"Is that an invitation?"

"What did I tell you about tired pickup lines?"

His laughter filled the stairwell. "That's right. You mentioned that. I will have to bring my best lines."

I laughed, too.

"I had a great time," I said to him.

Still smiling, he agreed. "Me too. We'll have to do this again, soon."

"You know where to find me."

He stared at me.

"You can't kiss me again," I said.

He scoffed in response. "That's presumptuous of you."

I laughed. "What's on your mind?"

"Is it a cheesecake night, or a rum one?"

I beamed. Kevin brought his hand to my face and held it. I was shocked by how good it felt.

"You are so fucking pretty," he said.

"You are kind of handsome yourself."

"I'm leaving," he said as he dropped his hand.

"Okay. You be safe out there."

"Of course," he said. "I'll call you."

"Okay. Good night," I softly said.

I let myself in and closed the door. I listened for footsteps descending the stairs. When I heard them echo away, I let out a breath.

"Marta; be careful with that one," I whispered to myself.

Still, I smiled as I retired to my bedroom for the night.

Chapter Twelve

I needed to clean so that my brain could travel. Hopefully, an investigative path for Doña Elena's niece would present itself. Wanting a space to tidy, I made my way to Erickson Ventures Chicago.

After letting myself into the office, I looked at Melissa's desk. It was unoccupied, even though it was working hours. She wasn't traveling for work, though, but was in Hanover, Pennsylvania, visiting family. I was proud of her.

I looked at Niels' office and saw the open door. The lights were off, which meant that he'd not yet made it in.

I began to clean. I started with the high surfaces - shelves, bookcases, and light fixtures. I even wiped down the light switches. After, I hit up Melissa's desk. I scoured all of the windows, using the lemon-scented cleaner she was so fond of.

I moved onto the men's bathroom. It had only one user, and Niels appeared to be a clean man. Leaving his bath, I made it to Melissa's. The distraction allowed me to get lost in thought, thankfully.

If the DNA testing website was to be believed, Doña Elena was related to at least 900 people.

"We come from the same mountain towns. I expect that when you test, that you'll find that you are related to as many people as I - if not more," she'd said during our bakery conversation. *"I bet that you and I are distantly related, which means that you would be related to her, too. That would be a good 'in' for you getting to know my niece."*

A confirmed DNA match between Doña Elena's niece Edna and I would be a good jumping-off point. I was supposed to be receiving my DNA test through the mail within the next couple of days. I would do the gross spitting thing and would pay for express decoding of my DNA.

"Not quickly enough," I muttered as I wiped down the windowsill in the bathroom.

I could not rely on a DNA test match to get close to the niece. Who knew what DNA testers thought about meeting people in real life? I had to get closer to her in a way that was independent of DNA testing.

Edna Nazario was Doña Elena's niece's name, and she was purported to be a dental technician somewhere in Greater Chicago. I would have to do some internet sleuthing at home. Perhaps I'd hit up some dental office websites later. Maybe I'd get lucky and would find Edna's name listed as an employee.

Plan set, I moved onto Mr. Erickson's office. I dusted his shelves, and I scoured his windows and windowsills. I climbed on a small ladder and dusted the light fixtures.

"You are thorough," I heard an accented voice say.

Still standing on the ladder, I turned to face the doorway. Mr. Niels Erickson stood there. His hands were in his pockets as he leaned on the door jamb. He looked like he had all the time in the world.

I descended the ladder and turned to face the doorway. "Good morning, Mr. Erickson. How are you?"

"I am well," he said. His English, while perfect, was slightly accented. It probably didn't bother him, nor did it anyone else. He was European - Danish, to be precise. He stood out, literally and figuratively, as he was quite tall and very fit. He had thick, dark hair that grayed at the sides just so. His light blue eyes were piercing. Sharp cheekbones framed his very handsome face.

Mr. Erickson was polite, but something was afoot. He looked reserved, perhaps even a touch put out.

"I won't be long, Mr. Erickson."

"Call me Niels. Please."

I blushed again. "Niels. Yes. It won't be long. I'll be out of your hair in no time."

"There is no rush."

For a moment, I awkwardly stood there. I was in Mr. Erickson's workspace. He wasn't working; he was just standing there and staring at me. Not knowing what else to do, I went back to cleaning. I dusted the back of his chair and then the chair legs.

"That is thorough - dusting the chair that way. Don't you find that unnecessary?"

I stood up and dusted my knees. "Some might think so. But, I like to consider the 'what-if's.' What if someone were to sit on your floor? Or fall. They might look around and find dust on your chair. I like leaving spotless spaces. I think that a clean space lets someone know that they are in control of it."

He nodded. "I appreciate that. It is good thinking."

Niels made me feel antsy and nervous, and I wished he would just go away. He could even go and take a dump in the freshly-cleaned bathroom. After all, nothing attracted a man's butt like a clean toilet.

Still, he stood there.

I let out a quiet breath and plugged the vacuum into an outlet in the wall. I pulled the cord behind me and made my way to the far corner of his office.

"Melissa is on vacation," he said.

Fuck, fuck, fuck, I thought to myself.

"She is," I said as I turned to face Niels.

"Melissa was only to go for three days. She called me and extended her vacation for two more days. That will make her absent for five days."

I might be a maid, but I could do basic arithmetic. If he weren't a paying client, I probably would have had choice words for him. But, I had rent to pay. Also, I wanted to remain employed at Erickson Ventures so that I could keep an eye on Melissa.

I suspected that my friendship with Melissa was probably pissing Niels off. Still, I stared at him.

He gave me a slow smile. "Have you no answer for me?"

"I didn't hear a question, Mr. Erickson."

His eyes shined brightly, and his smile widened. He was glowing. I realized what I'd done - I had intrigued him. That was not a good idea.

"No, I didn't. You are a smart apple, Marta. Is that the expression?"

I nodded. "It is. What are you asking of me, Mr. Erickson?"

"Did you advise Melissa to go and visit her family?"

Nervously, I squeezed the handle on the vacuum. I thought about the location of my cell phone, which was in my right pocket. Kevin was on my speed-dial. My pepper spray was in my left pocket. Also, the crystal paperweight on Niels' desk would probably work well as a weapon, too.

"It came up," I finally said.

He nodded and stood up straight.

"I need her here in the office."

"I can appreciate why. Melissa is a great worker."

He nodded. "She is. I think I might have to call her and tell her to come home early."

Niels was an asshole. Shoving down feelings of anger, I looked at his desk. I saw pictures of his wife, son, and daughter.

"Comfort is good. I think she's having a good time in Pennsylvania."

"Maybe," he said as he shrugged.

I stared at him a bit. "Family is everything. Wouldn't you agree with that?"

He blinked a few times. "I would."

I nodded. "I am sure you'll do what you think is best."

Niels opened his mouth to speak again. Having enough of his psychopathic talk, I looked him in the eye and then turned on the vacuum. I then gave him my back and began to vacuum.

Niels was throwing his weight around, and it was making me nervous. Ignoring him was a simple stand I could make. A future confrontation might not be so safe for me, though.

When I finished vacuuming the backside of his office, I turned to face the doorway. Niels was gone. Glancing at the lobby and Melissa's desk, I saw that he wasn't there, either. I looked towards the bathroom but did not hear water running nor the loud fan.

"Good God," I said as I let out a breath.

I quickly got through the rest of my cleanings for the day. Even Jane remarked on my sensitive nature.

"It's nothing," I said as I scrubbed the inside of her microwave. "I just...stepped on some toes. I was corrected. I will be keeping my mouth shut from here on out."

Jane continued staring at me. "Let me know if you need help with anything."

"I will, thank you," I said to her with a smile before turning back to the microwave.

I needed to keep my mouth shut about Niels and Melissa. Was I playing the puppet master with Melissa's life? Maybe I was. Who was I to play big brother - or big sister to her? I didn't have the right. Also, I did not need to make an enemy out of Niels.

With that in mind, I made it a point to focus on finding Edna Nazario - Doña Elena's niece. After showering and putting some sweats on, I sat at my computer and searched for dental offices in the Greater Chicagoland area. When I got ten pages worth of results, I refined my search criteria. A search for Edna Nazario and dental offices in Chicago yielded fewer results.

I was twenty minutes into my search when my cell rang. Without taking my eyes from the laptop screen, I answered the phone.

"Hello?"

"*¡Amiga!*" Melissa's voice happily said.

I smiled and turned away from the screen. "Hello! How is Pennsylvania?"

"We call it 'P.A.' over here. Pennsylvania has a lot of syllables in it."

I laughed. "Thank you for the local lingo tip."

She laughed, too.

"How's your vacation?"

"Well, I had been having fun, but then Niels called me with an emergency. So, I'm on my way back."

My smile faded. "Oh. When were you supposed to leave?"

"The day after tomorrow. I was going to try to extend the vacation for a couple more days, but Niels said that there's a need for me and that I could go back to P.A. in the fall. So, that's that. I'm at the airport in Harrisburg."

I scratched my nose as I considered what to say. I glanced at the door leading to the outside of my apartment. My home was small, but I had control over who entered it. My friend appeared to have little control over what was happening in her life.

"I can't wait to see you," I said, forcing cheer into my voice.

"That's the spirit!" she said as she laughed. "When can we get drinks again?"

Ten minutes later held me pouring myself a shot of rum, with no cheesecake on the side, because I wasn't celebrating.

I was relearning how to mind my own business. It sucked.

Chapter Thirteen

I resumed my search for Edna the following afternoon. It was surprisingly fruitful - perhaps suspiciously so. Already, I'd located about ten Edna Nazarios in the Greater Chicagoland area. Four of them were dental assistants.

"What is it about Ednas and their love of dental work?" I muttered.

It then occurred to me that maybe there was only one Edna Nazario and that perhaps she worked out of multiple offices. Maybe she was a job-switcher, and some of the locations had not updated their websites.

I groaned and let out a breath. I would have to investigate in person, it seemed. I couldn't just walk in those offices, though. I'd need to operate under the guise of needing dental work.

I reached for my purse and pulled my compact mirror from it. I took a good look at my mouth. I needed to touch up my lipstick, and the peach fuzz over my lip was looking a bit prominent. Were those hairs getting darker? Darned forties.

"Focus," I said as I stared at my teeth. I looked at my incisors, canines, and a couple of my molars.

"Damn," I muttered. While in Puerto Rico, I'd had a full exam, a cleaning, and a filling. Dental work was cheaper over there, which meant that I had no actual need to visit with a local dentist.

I set my compact down and looked at my computer screen again. Edna Nazario was listed as one of the dental assistants. A light bulb went off when I saw that they did cosmetic dental work. Perhaps I could go in for a bleaching consultation.

"No time like the present," I said as I reached for my phone.

I stared at the website, wondering how to time my appointment so that I could see Edna Nazario. I had to go for a busy day, I knew. I dialed the number and waited to speak to someone.

"Visions of Teeth dental office. This is Mayra speaking. How can I help you?"

"Hi. My name is Marta. I need some dental work. I think?" I was sure to inject a healthy amount of doubt into my tone, as I wanted to leave myself open for more information and upselling.

"Sure thing," Mayra enthusiastically said. "Can you come in for a consultation? It's free."

"I don't know," I said as I sighed. "I...don't have insurance, so I'd have to pay cash. I have to see what I can afford and what I cannot."

"We offer financing here, Marta, and we offer a cash discount. We are willing to do what we need to to give you a beautiful smile."

"Well, how about an evaluation? What days are good for that?"

"Tuesdays and Wednesdays are our busiest days. We can get you in sooner if you come in on a Monday, a Thursday, or a Friday."

I wrote the 'busy days' down on a pad.

"Okay. What if I just want bleaching or something like that? What if I don't do anything at all? Do you charge for that?"

"No," she drew out. "Of course not. We want to make you as comfortable as possible. Dental work is scary!"

I smiled. "It is. Okay. How does January 5th sound?"

"Well, that's a Tuesday. Our busiest day. Can you come in on a Thursday?"

I groaned. "You know what? I'm kind of busy. How about I call you back?"

Still, I wrote down Tuesday, January 5th, on my pad.

"If Tuesday works for you, then we'll make it work for us. Can I have your phone number, Marta?"

"Sure thing, Mayra."

After getting off the phone, I noted my research time in the file for Doña Elena. I also added to it the cost of gas, parking, and maybe even a tooth bleaching.

"A good start," I said as I let out a breath and stretched.

About two hours later, my phone rang again. I set down my half-eaten banana and took the call.

"¿Puedo hablar con Señorita Marta?" asked an accented voice.

I laughed out loud. "Why am I not surprised that you can speak some Spanish?"

"Because I am a police detective out of Chicago, Illinois," said Kevin.

"Your Spanish is good, I'll have you know."

"I'll take it as a compliment."

"I'd better be careful around you," I said as I dumped the banana peel in my trash can.

"That's the smart move," he said as he laughed. "But why?"

"Because you speak more Spanish than what you've let on," I said as I leaned on my counter.

He chuckled. "Damn. Maybe I should have kept that a secret a while longer."

I laughed out loud. "Maybe, but then again, I might have been able to determine your fluency through other methods."

He laughed again. "Please. Tell me how."

I smiled and walked to my living room, where I sat on the couch. "Okay. I think I can tell when people understand Spanish - or English - depending on the conversation."

"How do you do that?"

"If I am out at a restaurant or a store and people are talking in English, but stop what they are saying once I speak Spanish, I wonder. Sometimes I'll say a good joke to see if they react."

"Does that work?"

"Sometimes."

"You are too smart."

"Is that a problem?"

"No, Ma'am."

"We are going to have a problem if you call me 'ma'am' again," I said.

He laughed again. "I can't have that. My apologies, Miss Morales."

"Apology accepted." I then let out a breath and sat down on a chair in my kitchen. "Tell me about your day," I asked of him.

Kevin shared a couple of cases that he described as boring. He talked about some other police officers before telling me that he was tired and at home.

"How was your day?" he asked of me.

I let out a breath. There was no way I could tell him about my sleuthing. I was unlicensed, after all. Also, I suspected that the good detective might not approve of my moonlighting gig.

"I had a weird day," I confessed.

"How so?" he asked.

"One of my cleaning clients. He pays me very well and is very respectful and courteous. Stays out of my way."

"So?"

I let out another breath. "I work for this client in a professional capacity - in that I clean his business office, but not his home."

"Okay."

"But I'm getting the feeling that he pays more attention to things than I thought."

"What things? What specifically?" Kevin asked, all humor gone from his tone.

"He observes my behavior. I think he can sleuth me."

The detective was quiet for a bit.

"Do you feel threatened?"

I did.

"No," I replied.

I couldn't give up the gig. It was good money, and Melissa and Niels gave me my space. Also, I could keep an eye out for Melissa.

"I don't think you are truthful," Kevin said. "You are smart. You are cautious. If this guy's attention to you caught your notice, there's a reason for that."

"You are a good detective," I complimented.

"Don't try to distract me," he said, and quite severely.

"Now that was kind of sexy, Detective," I added as I smiled.

He laughed out loud. "Was it now?"

"Yes."

"Stop distracting me," he said. "Do you feel like you are in danger?"

I let out a breath. "No. I think the client's curious about me and what I do. But he's a married man and has kids. Is a good boss to my friend, who is his employee."

"Ah. Melissa Bollinger. Would this be Niels Erickson you are speaking of?"

Damn and damn. I did not need the detective sticking his nose into my professional life.

"I need you to leave this alone, Kevin," I said.

"Why?"

"Because I do. Okay? Will you leave it alone?"

He was quiet for a bit. "I have mixed feelings about this."

I sighed. "I understand. But I need this job. Niels is a smart, smart man. I don't need trouble. I only wanted to share the awkward exchange I had with him today."

"But you didn't do that!" he angrily said. "You didn't tell me what he said."

"Stop it!"

"What did I say?"

"I need you to be...my friend. My...special friend? My gentleman caller? Not a detective."

He laughed. "We have to dissect the first part of that statement first."

"No, we don't," I whined.

"But we do. Do you have a problem with the word BOYFRIEND?" he loudly said.

"Shhh," I said. "Don't say that!"

He laughed. "Why not? BOYFRIEND!" he yelled.

"Oh, dear Lord," I said as I paced my kitchen. "Don't say that! You aren't my boyfriend!"

"Why not?"

"Because that label signifies a relationship. We've only gone on one date!"

"We've gone on TWO dates, AND we've kissed."

Damn it. Kevin was kind of right. A few months ago, we'd shared lunch. He was supposed to have been questioning me, but he had decided to put that off as he didn't want to ruin our meal.

"Okay. We've had two dates, but you stole that kiss."

"Like a thug," he drawled.

I let out a breath. "Just don't call me your girlfriend. You haven't merited that yet."

"We are having our first fight. We are *definitely* boyfriend and girlfriend."

I groaned and then laughed. "You are incorrigible."

"I am persistent," he stated.

"You also left me hanging at the airport," I added.

77

Kevin groaned. "Fuck. I'll never live that down. See? That's something you can lord over me. If we weren't boyfriend and girlfriend, you couldn't lord anything over me."

"That doesn't make sense."

"I'm running with it."

I sighed. "Look. I need you not to be a detective on this, okay?"

"You know I can't shut that kind of thinking off. It doesn't work that way," he said, conviction filling his tone.

"I need you to try. Cleaning and keeping my clients happy is how I make a living, Kevin."

He groaned. "Fine. Fine. I won't forget about this weird guy, but I'll put off looking into him. For now."

"Just as long as you warn me."

"Can do," he said. "Now. I can respect the fact that you don't want me to call you my girlfriend. How about I called you my '*beba*' and you can call me your '*papi chulo*?'"

Kevin was incorrigible, persistent, and hilarious. I agreed to a second (or third, depending on who was counting) date with him, just as long as he never called me '*beba*.' He made no promises. I was alright with that.

Chapter Fourteen

One of the perks of being a maid was observing people. They interested the heck out of me. I loved it when they were normal, and I loved it when they were weird.

But weird could be too weird, especially if the odd behavior came from someone who'd previously been sphinxlike in their self-control.

"Good Morning, Marta!" Jane exclaimed as she opened the kitchen door for me.

I let out a breath. "Hello, Jane. How are you?"

"I am good! Great! I am trying a new kombucha drink. Have you ever had them?"

I shook my head as I removed my coat and hung it on a peg by the door. "I have not."

"Would you like some?" she asked.

Just then, Tim Peterson, her husband, entered the kitchen. He was smiling. "Hello, Marta! How are you?"

I nodded. "Good. How are you?"

"Great," he said to me. "Now, honey," he said to Jane. "You know Marta's a coffee gal. Aren't you?" he asked as he turned to me.

I nodded. "I am, but I appreciate the drink offer."

"Let me know if you change your mind," Jane said as she smiled at me.

"I will. I think I'll get started with the office this morning, just in case either of you wants to work from home today."

"That's great thinking," Tim said.

I departed the asylum greeting area and made my way to the closet that held my cleaning gear. From there, I went to the office. Once the door was closed, I let out a breath.

I walked to the desk and discreetly glanced at the calendar. I didn't know what I was looking for, but it was a place to start.

"Hmm," I said as I spotted a big clue. Until a day ago, Tim Peterson had been out of town.

I lifted my head and looked out of the glass office door to the kitchen beyond. Jane's behavior differences might be attributed to her husband's absences.

"But how?" I whispered.

I looked to the other things on the desk, on the windowsill, and the bookcases, but saw nothing that might indicate Jane's mood swings.

"Ah, well," I said. I carried on with cleaning the office and then the rest of the condo. My efforts rendered a clean home and effusive praise, but not more clues as to what was afflicting my boss/client.

Erickson Ventures Chicago was my next stop. I looked forward to seeing Melissa again.

"Time to carry on with the weirdness," I said.

I needn't have worried. While Niels Erickson was a Grade A psychopath, Melissa's was a breath of fresh air.

"It's so nice to see you!" she exclaimed.

I beamed. "Likewise. Are you busy?"

She shook her head. "No. I just got off a conference call. I'll keep you company while you dust."

"Sounds like a plan."

I worked on the high shelves in the waiting area while she sat down on a couch.

"So how was P.A.?"

"South Central P.A. is...South Central P.A. It doesn't change much. It's kind of comforting, though."

"That's great. How's the family?"

"Good," she said as she smiled. "My mom's the Cuban one, as you know. Dad's the one from P.A. He talks about moving south to Florida, where it's warm. Mom's not hearing it."

"Really?" I asked as I laughed. "Why not?"

"She says that crazies like warm weather."

I laughed out loud.

"Mom says that they can avoid the unhinged if they stay in P.A. Also, she likes the cold."

"What do you think? Could you ever see yourself moving back there?"

She let out a breath and pursed her lips. "You know, I used to think I could not. But now? I don't know. Maybe it's maturity. Maybe it's Chicago and not being around family. I think I could do small-town living again, which is what Hanover is – compared to Chicago."

"That's great."

"What? Aren't you going to force me to stay in Chicago? You'd miss me."

"Terribly so! But I would be happy picturing you in a small town. Close to family. Maybe building a small family of your own."

I then noticed how quiet Niels' office was. Had he been eavesdropping? Probably. Still, I carried on as if he wasn't.

"Puerto Rico keeps changing. Not a shocker, I know. But it catches me off guard. I come off the plane and come home to something familiar yet new."

"Can you see a life for yourself – if you had to move back?"

Having completed my dusting, I climbed off the stool and turned to face her. "I don't. I don't see a spot where I can fit there. Not anymore."

Her phone rang. "Hold on."

"I'll move to the bathrooms," I whispered.

Melissa nodded and then sat down at her desk. I took a breath and stepped into Niels' doorway, where I saw him at his desk, quietly typing away. Was he fake typing? Was he submitting some kind of psychopath manifesto?

"Mr. Erickson?" I asked.

He stopped typing and looked up at me. "Marta. Hello. Are you well?"

"I am, Sir. Thank you for asking. I'll move onto your bathroom now if that's alright with you."

"Of course."

"If you'll excuse me," I said as I ducked out of his doorway and headed for the bathroom.

After cleaning Mr. Erickson's bathroom, I moved on to the ladies' room. I wasn't there long before Melissa joined me.

"Drinks again! When can we do that?" she asked as she sat down on the bench.

"What works for you?"

"How about Saturday night?"

I cringed. "I...can't. I have a date."

"WHAT? WHAT??!!," she shrieked.

I laughed and told her about Detective Kevin Connelly.

"Oh my goodness!" she said as she beamed. "That's so awesome! I am so thrilled for you."

I shrugged. "It might be soon for excitement, but I'm having fun. Kevin's fun."

She lifted her eyebrows. "How about the other detective? Detective Kostas?"

I laughed. "How do you remember Detective Kostas' name?"

"Because your life is exciting!"

I laughed and finished cleaning the toilet.

"Spill the beans!" she demanded.

I wiped down the mirror before speaking. "Detective Kostas strikes me as a man who is not ready to be into one woman. If you know what I mean."

I looked at Melissa and saw that she was blushing.

"I get what you mean. But what about Detective Connelly?"

I beamed. "Um. Well. Kevin is more receptive to the thought of dating just one woman. He is ready to have fun and to smile and laugh."

"A great start!"

"I think so," I replied.

I finished cleaning the bathroom and moved onto Niels' office, which was vacant, thankfully. After, I hit up Melissa's work area.

"I am going to buzz you later to find out about a day where we can go out for drinks."

"Please do," I said.

I stored my cleaning gear and was getting ready to head for the door. Melissa stared at me.

"Are you happy to be back?" I asked of her.

She blinked a few times before answering. "This is where I work. I have obligations here. Friends," she added.

I laughed as I considered something.

"What?"

"Do you think that Cubans and Puerto Ricans share the same expressions?"

"Let's find out."

"Te conozco bacalao," I said.

Her reaction - tear-filled eyes and lots of nods - alerted me to her familiarity with the expression indicating that the speaker knew that the other person was hiding something.

"I know the idiom," she finally said.

"You know where to find me," I said to her.

I was somber as I left Erickson Ventures. I got the sense that Melissa knew that Niels was trying to tighten his leash on her, but I wasn't sure if she was ready to do anything about it. Still, her love for her family and the easy life of her home state meant something.

Giving me an odd sense of comfort were the two residential customers I had. They ignored me, and I ignored them. I deliberately overlooked the contents of their trash cans and what covered their nightstands and their dressers. I did not read refrigerator lists, nor did I look at sticky notes on computer monitors. I didn't spy how many sets of keys sat on console tables or hung from hooks on the wall. I just cleaned. I said goodbye, they said goodbye, and that was that.

One the way home, I stopped by a *colmado* to get some cheesecake and rum. Jane Knight and Melissa Bollinger's personal lives were twisting my insides into knots. It was not my job to clean up or reorganize their personal lives - as much as I wanted to. So, I tended to my own life.

My mother called me that night.

"Hi, Mom," I said as I hit pause on my DVR. I had been catching up on a police procedural TV show.

"Hi. How are things?"

I let out a breath. "Good. Cleaning. Hanging out. Living through a Chicago winter. How are things over there?"

"Van bien. Good. How's your investigation for Doña Elena?"

I smiled. "Mom - she's a client. I can't divulge that information to you."

"Of course, you can! I am your mother! I help you."

I nodded. "And you are of great help to me. How about this? If I need you to do some picking around there, I'll let you know."

"I can help you now."

"You cannot, Mom. There's nothing worth wasting your time over right now," I placated. "You're a busy woman; you take care of dad, help with Rafy's kids, and you do the stuff with the church and all of your siblings. I'm surprised you have time for yourself."

"Well, I don't," she asserted. "Just yesterday, your Aunt Josefa asked me to come over so that I could give her an opinion on a couch set she bought. But why does she need my opinion? Josefa already *bought* it! What kind of answer was she expecting? Of course, I *had* to tell her that she had great taste..."

I felt kind of bad manipulating my mom's attention like that. I alleviated my guilt by telling myself that I was lending her an ear. I half-listened to her while I stared at my television, wondering what the less-than-comely, middle-aged police detective would do to find the guy who'd stolen the diamonds from the young and pretty oil heiress. The heiress was hitting on the detective, which made her look more guilty.

"Inside job," I accidentally muttered aloud.

"What?" Mom asked. "What did you say?"

I abruptly sat up straight. "Nothing, Mom. Just saying that Tia Josefa's old couches being ruined was probably an inside job."

"That's what I said!" was her reply. Mom then picked up where she left off.

I couldn't help but let my mind travel. Mom was deep into her monologue. If I were in Puerto Rico, how long would I have to listen to that conversation? Could I have begged off? Would I have to hear it in person? Could I pull out a newspaper and feign interest, like my dad would have done? Or maybe look at my phone like my brother Rafy was known to do?

Suddenly, I felt like a heel. Who listened to my mom? Did others disregard her conversation as much as I did? Did people take her for granted? Tears filled my eyes, and I forced myself to listen to her.

"...but he won't buy me new couches. He says that these are just fine."

"They are good-looking couches, Mom. Didn't you say you wanted a new dining set anyway?"

"Yes! I do. But, this one works fine, too," she said.

I noticed that she sounded a bit more enthusiastic. Maybe she could tell that I was paying attention to her.

"Mom?"

"Yeah."

"I visited Anibal. Want to hear about it?"

"Yes! Of course, I do!" she excitedly said.

So, I told her. She was sympathetic about mine and Anibal's difficulties with our son's ex-wife. She was proud of me for treating my ex-husband with kindness and respect.

"What are you going to do? Approach Waleska?"

"The truth is that I am kind of scared. Waleska has all the power."

Mom let out a breath. "I can see that. But you have to try."

"I think I will. Thanks for listening to me."

She cleared her throat. "Of course. That is what I am here for. I am always here."

"Thanks, Mom."

I stared at my cell phone long after I'd ended the call. I wondered if all mother-daughter relationships were complicated. I remembered how I told Hector that I would always be there for him. Letting out a breath, I scrolled through my contacts before finding the number I was looking for. I let out a sigh and then hit the green handset button.

"Hello?" inquired a Spanish-accented voice.

"Hello? Cleofe? This is Marta Morales. Hector's mother?"

I hadn't addressed myself aloud like that in a while. Of course, I was still Hector's mother. That would never change. Damn tears. I dried them and continued.

"Hello, Marta," she kindly said. "How are you?"

I let out a breath of relief. "Same old, same old. How are you?"

"Ay, Marta. My husband, Victor, has cancer. He is on his way out."

"I am so sorry to hear that, Cleofe."

I listened to her tell me about her husband and how long he'd been ill. After, I got to the reason while I was calling her.

"Cleofe? I am calling because I wanted to know how to reach Waleska."

"Okay. But...why do you need to?"

I let out a slow, calming breath. "I want to see how Waleska's doing. I want to see my grandson."

"Adan is fine and well-loved. Don't you worry."

Instantly, I stood up. "Is Waleska still living Cobblewood Towers?"

"I don't feel comfortable telling you that."

Damn it, I mentally cursed. I paced while I thought of what to say next.

"Cleofe? Thank you for your time. Don't let me keep you from Victor any longer."

"Marta," she quickly asked. "What are you going to do?"

"I am going to get ready for work tomorrow. But you take care of yourself and say hello to Victor. Good night, now."

"Marta!"

I hung up and then threw my cell phone at a couch cushion.

"Damn it!" I cussed. I tried holding back tears but then wondered why. I sat down on my couch and had a good cry.

Letting go felt good. Not that it was helpful. Having nothing else to do, I did what I told Cleofe what I was going to do – I got ready for the next day's work.

Chapter Fifteen

Three days had passed since I'd spoke to Cleofe - Waleska's mother. I'd allowed her to cow me into not getting in contact with my grandson's mother.

Ashamed and depressed, I dressed for my date with Kevin. We were going to see a movie and would have dinner after.

"Did I tell you that you look nice?" He asked.

His European luxury car smelled of leather and cleanliness. I liked it.

"You did. Thank you."

I put some effort into my outfit. Under my long jacket, I wore a black blouse and black slacks with boots underneath. I let my hair do its thing and used a light hand when applying my makeup, too.

Kevin kept sneaking glances at me, even while he drove.

"Oh, I'm sorry. Did I not compliment you on your dress? You look handsome tonight."

He chuckled. "Thank you."

"Is that why you were staring?"

"Nope," he said as he looked out at the traffic again.

"What is it?"

"You're down. It's not like you."

I let out a breath. "I'm not bubbly, Detective."

He laughed. "I didn't say you were. I am just saying that you are down, and it shows."

"That's fair."

"Care to tell me what's on your mind?"

I considered it. "Well, sure. But you have to promise not to do anything about what I am going to tell you."

"Good God, Marta! Again?!"

"Again, what?" I whined.

He scoffed. "You've asked me not to do anything about a probable psychopath you work for. Now, something else is bothering you that might be against the law?"

"No. It's not like that."

"That is what you are making it sound like. You prefacing statements with 'promise not to do anything' raises all sorts of red flags. Like...maybe you get into stuff you are not supposed to. Like...continually."

He was closer to the truth than I liked.

"Fine, fine," I repeated. "I might have to sue someone for something. I don't want to do that."

"Who? Why?!" he said as he whipped his head my way.

"My son's widow. I'm scared she's trying to keep my grandson from me. I've been looking into grandparents' rights. I don't want it to have to come to that - getting the court involved."

Kevin let out a breath. "Well. Wow."

"I know. I called Cleofe - that's Waleska's mom - but she won't give me information on her daughter. She's trying to discourage me from getting in contact again."

"Waleska? Cleofe?" Kevin said.

I nodded. "Yeah. Waleska was my daughter-in-law, and Cleofe is her mom."

"You won't have to worry about me looking those names up, because there's no way I'd remember them anyway."

I smiled. "Fair enough. Waleska is somewhat common in Hispanic countries. Cleofe - a traditional name like Mildred - has fallen out of favor."

"I can't imagine why."

I laughed, and then he did, too.

"Do you want me to advise you?"

"Yeah. Yes," I said as I turned to face the detective.

"Don't assume anything. Just because your son's...mother-in-law doesn't want you to reach out does not mean that your daughter-in-law does not. But keep an attorney's number on standby. Things could get ugly."

"That's what I'm afraid of."

"Don't be. That's your grandson. You should be a part of his life."

"I know," I softly said.

"Go for an easy approach. Write your daughter-in-law a letter - a polite one devoid of threats or guilt."

"That sounds like a safe move."

"You want to play this safe."

"I do."

I was lost in thought for the remainder of our drive, and even as we entered the movie theater. Kevin seemed to respect my silence, which I was grateful for. Perhaps it was because I told him what was weighing on me.

I might have been too lost in thought, though.

"Wait. What are we watching?" I asked as we approached the doors to a theater room.

"1906. The Hitless Wonders. You know - World Series, the White Sox, and the Cubs."

"Kevin! That's so boring!"

His blue eyes expanded. "Are you kidding me? This is great stuff!"

I groaned and looked at the other theaters. "There's a werewolf movie playing over there. And the next room is showing a prison break movie. And there's a comedy about British royalty. Why didn't you pick one of those?"

"You said you didn't care!" he argued.

I let out a breath. "Darn. Alright. Fine. Let's see it."

"Now, that makes me feel bad."

"No. We'll watch your movie. It might be good."

Kevin smiled. "It will be. You'll see."

The movie sucked. While watching it, I came up with ideas on what to say in a letter to Waleska. I'd ask her how she was doing and would tell her that I would love the opportunity to visit with her and Adan. I would apply no pressure.

After mentally composing the letter, I moved on to thinking about my upcoming dental consult. There's no way I could get my teeth bleached, as that was too expensive. I doubted that one visit would be enough to get the information I needed on Edna Nazario. Also, I needed to learn the real reason why Doña Elena was looking for her.

I recalled that I'd not yet checked my mail with Doña Justa. My DNA spit kit was supposed to have arrived. I needed to figure out how much spit I would need to supply, and how long I needed to fast before contributing it.

As heartbreaking as it was, I'd have to start looking for a business client that was not Erickson Ventures Chicago. Walking the line between being Melissa's friend and her employee was hard. Also, there was the fact that her boss was creepy.

"Darn," I said out loud.

"I know," Kevin whispered. "But they get it back here in the end. You'll see."

Kevin thought I was reacting to the movie. I let him run with that. When it was over, I let out a breath of relief.

"Did you like it?" he asked.

"Did you?" I countered.

"Don't answer a question with a question," he said as he got up.

I sighed and stretched. "If you enjoyed it, I am glad. Honest."

And I was. Kevin worked hard and was excited to see the movie. I would not ruin that for him.

He kept staring at me. "You didn't like it."

"No. I'm sorry."

"Are you?"

"Are you trying to pick a fight because of my opinion of this movie? I was quiet! I didn't demand that we change our tickets. I said that I was glad that you enjoyed it. But, if you insist on learning my less-than-polite opinion, I'll share." I took a breath and continued. "Oh, my goodness. They should have left that movie in

1906. They should have left the werewolf next door eat the film, or at least the script."

"Ouch, Marta!"

"You wanted to know!" I pontificated. "Also, have you seen how many other women are here in the theater?"

I looked around and motioned towards the seated people, the ones getting ready to leave, and the ones by the exit.

"There are like...three other women here. And like fifty guys. Do you think that's a coincidence?"

"It is not," chimed in a woman a couple of rows behind us. "I lost a bet to my husband," the middle-aged woman said of the popcorn-eating man seated next to her. "That's why I'm watching this shit-show of a movie."

I laughed out loud. "Thank you for that."

"Look, Sam, I got a 'thank you' from a stranger," the woman said to her husband. "So, there's that. Being that I'll never get the ninety minutes back that I wasted on this movie."

Her husband shook the bottom of his popcorn bag. "That's what you get when you challenge the warrior, Carla."

Kevin chuckled and let out a groan. "Fine. Fine. Let's go."

"What were you planning for dinner?" I asked as we made our way to the parking lot.

"Mexican," he said.

I shook my head. "No. Try again."

"Fine. What do you want?"

"Steak, I think. Maybe some cheesecake after?"

He pursed his lips. "Fine. It'll make up for my choice of a movie."

"I think it will."

Just like that, our night improved. Following a good meal and better conversation, Kevin drove me home.

"When are we doing this again?" he asked.

I turned to him. "Well, I have something to do tomorrow evening. It's kind of boring, but you can feel free to come along."

"Wow. How could I possibly turn that down?" Kevin dryly inquired.

I laughed. "It'll be free! And it might be fun. It will be educational."

"Tell me more."

"It's a talk at a library. A DNA expert and genealogist will be talking about mail-in DNA tests and how they connect to family trees."

Kevin nodded. "I will admit that that appeals to the detective in me. What else have you got to round out the boringness?"

I laughed. "Okay. After, we can come back to my place. I'll fry up some fritters for you, and we can share some of the light beer I imported from-"

"Done," he said, cutting me off. "You had me at beer. No," he amended, "you had me at fritters."

"It's a date," I said.

"Sure as heck," was his answer.

Kevin idled his car in front of the gate that controlled access to my walk-up.

"So. Can I get a good night kiss?"

I let out a breath. "A peck. No tongue."

"I'll take it," he said.

I had to admit that I was excited. Kevin leaned my way, and I leaned into him. His lips were soft but firm. They were warm, even as the cabin of his vehicle was on the cool side. He smiled and kissed me again.

"You like kissing me, Marta."

I laughed. "I don't hate it."

"I can read you like a book."

"Maybe. I have to go. Busy day tomorrow."

"When should I come to pick you up?"

"How about you meet me there? I have something to do before I make it to the library."

"What?"

"Cleaning stuff."

"Okay. Run on up. I'll watch you until you make it in the door."

"Good night."

"You too, Marta."

I couldn't stop smiling as I undressed and jumped in the shower. It was a good night.

Chapter Sixteen

An unscheduled and unrequested Jane Knight check-in was what I had to do before meeting Kevin.

"Hey. What are you doing here?" Jane asked. She'd been wiping down her counter.

I let out a breath. "I wanted to Easy-Off the oven tonight so that I could scrub it tomorrow."

"Isn't that a harsh cleaner?" she asked, her brow furrowing.

"Yes, but...every other green cleaner is a pain in the rear. Easy-Off gets the job done right and fast."

"I pay you for green cleaning - not the easy stuff with harsh chemicals."

I had my answer. Jane was within normal ranges. Interesting.

"Okay. Let me get my vinegar and baking soda from the car."

She stared at me a bit. "Wait a minute. Are you going to charge me extra because it will take you longer to scour my oven?"

I let out a breath. "If you were an hourly client, I would. But you are a flat rate one, so no."

"And rightly so. Use the green stuff."

Forty minutes later, the oven was covered in a sticky white substance. Jane had sat down at her table to read a magazine.

"You won't be able to use the oven until tomorrow evening," I said as I removed my gloves.

"What? Why?"

"It takes a while to get all of the baking soda out. It sits into the crevices and stuff."

"Why didn't you mention that before?"

I let out a slow breath. "I am sorry if I forgot that detail, Jane."

She rolled her eyes. "Whatever. Guess I'll have takeout tomorrow."

"Were you planning on cooking a big meal?"

"No. Tim's out of town."

Ah ha. More information.

"I'll have it cleaned up tomorrow."

"Yeah, yeah. Carry on with your evening. Do you have plans?" Jane asked as she lowered her magazine.

"Maybe."

"What? What are you doing?"

"I have a date."

Her mouth dropped open. "With whom?"

"A guy," I deflected.

"No, shit. Who is this guy?"

"Are you asking me in a friendly manner or a professional one?"

"What's it matter? The line is blurred anyway."

"True," I said as I let out a breath. "My date's a police detective."

Jane beamed - and she looked so pretty doing it.

"Is it one of the ones from before? The one that helped with Maria or *tried* to help find her?"

I laughed. "Yeah."

"Which one?" she asked as she clapped.

"How about you guess?"

"Yes. YES! My deductive reasoning is unmatched! But you'll have to give me a hint."

I thought about it. "Okay. My date is the detective that smiles more easily. Laughs more quickly, too."

She stared at me for a few seconds. "The ginger."

I laughed. "How could you tell?"

She scoffed. "Bald men have something to prove. Ginger folks develop a thick skin early on. They learn how to laugh things off sooner. They have good senses of humor."

I laughed. "Kevin is quick to laugh."

"Good for you," she said before lifting her magazine again.

"I'll see you tomorrow."

I moved to leave but was stopped.

"Marta?"

"Yeah, Jane?"

"You need to pester the detectives for an update on Maria Alvarez."

I let out another breath. "Can you do that for me?"

"No. I don't have another garage for you to clean out. You need to find out where the police department is on things, though."

"Fine," I said as I let out a breath. "Okay."

"Cool. Go away. Have a good date."

Happily, I did. Having already been dressed in casual date attire, I made my way to the library. I beamed just as soon as I saw Kevin's unmarked car. He was at my car door just as soon as I parked it.

"Can I greet you with a kiss?" He asked.

"A peck. No tongue."

"I don't think I want to tongue you in a parking lot."

"That sounds illicit."

"Because it is."

"Is not," I argued, but I smiled.

"Are you truly going to argue the law with me?" he asked as he grabbed my hip and pulled me closer to him.

"Maybe not right now. It's cold. Later?"

"How about you give me a kiss?"

"Okay."

He pecked me twice. His lips were warm, and now other parts of my body were warm, too.

"Why do you smell like vinegar? Have you had salt and vinegar chips?"

I groaned. "No. I had to stop by a client's house. I had to douse her oven in vinegar and baking soda."

"Why would you do that?"

"To clean it. Do I smell bad?"

"No. I like salt and vinegar chips."

"Good. Ready to go in?"

"Yeah. I'm freezing my butt off."

So, we went inside. We sat near the back while we waited for the other library patrons to fill the seats before us. We didn't have to wait long.

"Beware of at-home DNA tests!" warned our host - a middle-aged genealogist named April Lee. "You might get answers to questions you didn't know to ask. You'll even get answers to questions you didn't want to be answered," April said, her voice filled with gravitas.

Immediately, I was pulled in. I grabbed my notebook and pen and prepared to take notes. Kevin's brow furrowed as he glanced at it, but said nothing.

"How about I go ahead and pre-emptively answer some frequently asked questions? DNA tests will tell you who your parents might be, and who they might not be. They might tell you that you aren't Irish at all, but that you are Lithuanian."

"No," Kevin whispered.

I chuckled but kept my silence.

"DNA testing will teach you that secrets can no longer be taken to the grave."

I jotted that down and sat further on my seat.

"That is a boon for law enforcement. DNA has given them assistance in solving cases that have long gone cold. Your DNA," April said as she paced, "might help shake loose an unknown criminal from your family tree."

"No, we know those guys," said a man, making many in the audience laugh.

April Lee laughed, too. "Fair point. But Grandma's tale that you are distantly related to President Barack Obama might be ruined! You might learn that you are related to Rod Blagojevich."

"That's more fitting," said an older woman.

"You guys are a funny crowd," April Lee said as she smiled.

"And you are a talented raconteur," said an older gentleman.

April smiled. "Thank you. But yes - I do love storytelling. That's what genealogy is - pulling facts out of the air - and your spit - to form your life story and what came before you."

The genetic genealogy talk made for a great, entertaining hour - and enjoyable learning. I took a copious amount of notes, too. When it was over, I thanked April for her time, as did many others.

"Why were you taking so many notes?" Kevin asked as he walked me to my car.

"I...am going to do a DNA test. I am curious about what I'll be getting into before I submit my saliva to an unknown company."

"Smart. But why test yourself at all?"

"Curiosity."

"Hmm," he said. "Alright. I'll meet you at your place."

Forty-five minutes later held the detective seated at my kitchen table, and drinking a beer.

"Would there be any surprises in your DNA test?" I asked Kevin. I was frying a plantain/potato/seasoned ground beef/pepper concoction called *alcapurrias*.

Kevin laughed out loud. "No. Well...maybe. My parents came here from Ireland. My grandparents are still there. So, as far as ethnicity is concerned, there will be no surprises. However, Dad looks more like his uncle than he does his father."

I laughed out loud, as did Kevin.

"Yikes. Maybe you *shouldn't* do a DNA test."

"True story," he said as he had another sip of beer. "My grandparents have passed, now, so it wouldn't hurt them."

"Maybe their memories, though. Also, their kids - your cousins?"

"Yes. I have lots of those. So many."

"Me too," I said as I set a platter of fried *alcapurrias* on the table. I got a beer for myself and sat across from Kevin.

Kevin smiled as he stared at the plate.

"You are going to want to be careful. The *alcapurrias* are hot. A bit of an acquired taste-"

The good detective did not care. Using a napkin, he grabbed an *alcapurria* and had a bite. Immediately, his eyes widened as did his mouth. He blew hot air like a dragon of old.

"I told you it was hot."

"I'm hungry," he said, mouth full. "But damn; these are good."

"I'm glad you like them."

We ate a few more before I fried the pizza turnovers called *empanadillas de pizza*.

"Are you expecting any mysteries in your DNA test? In your family tree?" he asked of me.

"Not really. I'm Puerto Rican, so I expect to see that most of my DNA will be Spanish, with some Native American and African DNA in there, too. What I'm curious about is how many people I might be related to."

After frying the pizza fritters, I sat at the table again.

"How do you have room for all this food?" Kevin asked.

"I didn't eat lunch," I said as I smiled.

"Well, I did. But I can't stop eating," the detective whined.

"Then eat," I prompted.

Kevin kept staring. His blue eyes held mine.

"You took a lot of notes. Back at the library," he said.

I nodded. "I like doing my homework."

"Yeah, but you took notes in Spanish. Why did you do that?"

I cringed. "I didn't think you noticed that."

He shrugged. "It's what I do, Marta." He sat forward on his seat. "Here's what I think; I think you wrote those notes in Spanish because you didn't want me to understand them. I am pretty good at reading Spanish, because I do my homework, too."

I sighed. "Okay. Fine. Do you want me to tell you things?"

"Yeah. Sure. But more importantly...why the subterfuge? Because that made you look more suspicious. If you'd written your notes in English, I wouldn't have thought much about it."

I had to give Kevin something. Not too much, though, as he did not need to know about my side-job.

"Okay. A family friend is looking for a relative in Chicago. This family friend is distantly related to me. This family friend wanted to know if I could help find this distant cousin of hers. The chances are that I might be related to the Chicago-based cousin. Her DNA was tested. I want to see if I can reach out to her that way."

Kevin scratched at his neck. "Okay. But why doesn't this family friend approach her herself? Does she not speak English? Does the Chicago-based person not speak Spanish?"

"Doña Elena Matos - the distant cousin of mine - speaks English and Spanish. I don't know what this other cousin speaks. But I told her I would help her. She's an old family friend."

"This sounds sketchy."

I shrugged. "Maybe. But I wanted to help."

For money - I wanted to help because I was getting paid. Not that I would reveal that.

"Why didn't you want me to know about this? Why write your notes in Spanish?"

"Because I didn't want you to investigate stuff for me. I didn't want you to look into people."

"Why not?"

I shrugged. "I don't know. I'm private, I guess."

Kevin sat back. "We are trying to get to know each other, Marta. If you keep things from me...that's going to get in the way of building anything."

"I know, Kevin. I know," I said, starting to panic. "But this is new to me. I don't know how much to give you. I don't know what to share. I haven't dated in forever. And I'm getting older," I said as my voice cracked. "I don't know what's going to send you packing, or send me packing. I don't know, but I want to learn."

Kevin stopped my panicked arguments in his tried-and-true manner - by kissing me. I relaxed into it. He stopped before things got too heated, though.

"We'll take things as slowly as you need. Heck - as slow as I need."

"That works for me," I said, trying to catch my breath.

"Don't lie to me. I don't like lies."

"I don't share everything. That's hard. That will take time."

He nodded. "That's fine. Just as long as you share it sometime."

I let out a breath. "Okay. That works."

He kept staring at me. "You know; if I hadn't just eaten my weight in deep-fried food, I'd be putting the moves on you."

"That's a good pick-up line. You should hang onto that one."

He laughed out loud and hard. I did, too.

"In all seriousness," he said as he dried an eye, "the fried food will help absorb all the beer I've had. That beer is good. Light, but good."

"Yeah. Some of my cousins prefer it for breakfast, and not over lunch or dinner. They prefer Coors or Heineken as evening drinks."

The detective stared at me. "If I didn't have drunken cousins of my own, that might have freaked me out."

I laughed out loud that time. I saw Kevin to the door shortly after.

"Kevin?"

"Yeah."

"How's the search going? For Maria Alvarez?"

Keven let out a breath. "In progress. I have to check in with James to get the details. He's taken the lead on that again."

I nodded.

"You're safe, okay? He would have shared something otherwise."

I nodded. "Detective Kostas doesn't call me as much as he used to."

Kevin, who had been walking to the door, stopped and turned to face me. "Say what?"

I blushed. "James used to call me every other day or so. Just to check on me and give me Maria updates."

Kevin nodded and took a breath. "That's got to stop now."

"It was official business – the calls from before."

"I will officially debrief you from here on out."

"That sounds cheesy," I teased.

"I don't care," he asserted.

"Kevin; it's been a good date. Don't make James Kostas a thing."

He grumbled something and then let out a breath. "Fine. I'll talk to James about Maria. I'll bring you in if I need to."

I nodded. "I'd like that."

I opened the door for him. He leaned on the frame and looked down at me. "This was a good date, Marta. Everything. The library talk about DNA, the fried foods, and the confidences. This was good."

"Yeah?" I said.

"Yeah," he answered.

He leaned down and kissed me twice. "I'll text you tomorrow, okay?"

"Yeah."

"Good night, Marta."

"You too, Kevin."

He kissed me again and then left.

I should have gotten back to my notes on Doña Elena's case. Instead, I immersed myself in thinking about the wonderful night I'd had.

Chapter Seventeen

The reckoning would not wait. I thought I had more time. But, she would not stay away forever. She knew people, just like I did. She knew who to call. She knew when to strike, too - at night, when my defenses were down. She knew what to say to me, just as soon as she got me on the phone.

"Am I a good mother to you, Marta?" inquired Zoraida Mercado - a.k.a. - mom.

I let out a breath and sank onto my couch.

"Yes, Mom. You are a good mother."

"Good. Good. Thank you for saying that. I have made it my mission to be a good mother. Always. I am not perfect," she said, her voice starting to get a bit singsongy. "But who is? Not me. No. I am not perfect."

I closed my eyes and let out a breath. I kicked my shoes off, too, as I had to get comfortable. Zoraida Mercado had something to get off her chest, and she was going to take her time with it.

"Yes. My daughter lives in Chicago. I miss her," she said. "She lives so far away. How can I keep an eye on her when she lives so far? I cannot. But I *love*. I love so strongly - from far away. And I wish that my daughter could love me back."

"Mami, I do love you-"

"Shut up! I am talking here!" she snapped.

"Good God," I groaned.

"Don't you dare take that tone with me!"

"Sorry, Mom. You were saying?"

"Aha. Yes. I try to be a good mother. A supportive mother. A mother you can talk to. Can you imagine how hard it was for me to find out that my daughter has a boyfriend? A man I know nothing about?"

"Goodness. Who spilled the beans?"

"It doesn't matter who told me!"

"Doña Justa. It had to have been."

"It doesn't matter who!" she repeated.

"Alright, Mom," I said. "I am dating someone. He is a police detective named Kevin."

"What is his last name?"

"That's enough information, I think," I said as I made my way to the kitchen.

"Was this the man that picked you up from the airport?"

I scoffed. "No. Kevin did not pick me up from the airport."

"Is he a good man?"

I opened the cupboard above the stove, looking for my rum.

"I think I am done answering your questions."

"Why?"

I poured myself a shot and sniffed it. "Because I don't like the *way* you are asking me questions, Mom."

"How else would I know?" she demanded.

"By asking, Mom. Without the drama."

I threw back the shot.

"Okay. I will ask now. Nicely."

"No," I said as I set the shot glass back down on the counter. "It's too late for that."

"Are you drinking rum?!"

"I'm not answering that. And you weren't nice. This conversation is over."

I then quickly said goodbye and hung up. Mom called again, but I ignored it. It rang again.

"Momma's boy," I said as I stared at Rafy's number. I didn't take his call, either.

"Time to formulate some questions," I said as I pulled out the file I had for Edna Nazario.

Chapter Eighteen

It was time for my cosmetic dentistry consultation. I flossed and brushed the crap out of my teeth. I made sure that my face was clear of weird hairs, and that my nose was clean as well.

Making my way to Oak Park, where the dental office was, I wondered which kind of appointment I prepared for more - OB visits or dental ones.

"We women are vain creatures," I said as I turned into the parking lot of the Visions of Teeth. "What's with that name?" I muttered to myself.

I took a breath and made my way into the office. My first impressions were good ones. The waiting room was expensive. A plush carpet sat under contemporary/modern leather seats. A long tufted ottoman sat in the center. Current, uncreased magazines sat in holders along the walls. Charging stations were discreetly placed within the armrests of the chairs. A coffee bar sat off to the side. I made my way to a central desk.

"Good morning! Welcome to Visions of Teeth. Might you have an appointment?"

"I do. My name is Marta Morales," I said as I looked at the woman's nametag.

Ah. It was Mayra - the woman who took my call. I looked around at another woman sitting behind a desk, but could not read her nametag.

"Thank you for coming, Marta. Might you please complete these intake forms?"

"Sure thing," I said.

I took the time to scrutinize the form before making my way to the waiting area. "I don't have health insurance. I'll pay cash or credit. Will that be a problem?"

Mayra beamed. "Not at all."

I sat down with the clipboard and the complimentary pen provided by the helpful Mayra. I filled out my name but listed my recently-acquired post office box. Thankfully, it was an actual street address and not a box number. I did not list my social security number, either. I registered a credit card that had a one-hundred-dollar limit on it.

I kept an eye on the front desk. As soon as I saw Mayra leave, I grabbed the clipboard and made my way over there.

"Excuse me; do you want the forms back, or should I give them to the...hygienist?"

The dark-haired woman looked my way. Her name tag read Sylvia, unfortunately. "I can take it, Miss Morales," she said with a smile.

"Thank you," I said.

I made my way back to my seat and waited. I took the time to look at everyone else in the room. They looked distracted. Some stared at their cell phones while others read magazines. Mayra had not been wrong about the busyness of the day; the waiting room was full. Shortly after, I was called back.

"Miss Morales?" said a woman wearing a white lab coat.

I grabbed my purse and headed towards her. Spying her nametag, I saw that she was named Raquel. Darn it. Where was Edna Nazario?

I wondered how long I'd have to continue the farce for. Still, I faked a smile and made my way to a dental chair in an otherwise unoccupied room.

A woman in a white lab coat - this one named Nanette - walked in and smiled.

"Hi. I'm Nanette. I hear that you are interested in tooth bleaching?"

I let out a breath. "Maybe. I am not too sure. Maybe you can tell me more about it?"

"Okay," she said as she sat down on a wheeled stool. "Can you smile for me? Big?"

I laughed, and she did, too. "That never fails in getting folks to smile," she explained. "May I?" she asked as she showed me her glove covered hands.

"Sure," I answered.

Using her hands, she moved my lips around while she examined my teeth. She nodded and then sat back.

"Well, Marta. I hate turning away potential customers, but...your teeth look good."

I smiled. "That's good to know."

"What brings this on?" she asked as she pulled her gloves off and set them in a wastebasket. "The desire to brighten your smile."

The best lies were veiled truths, I knew. "My boyfriend is younger than me. He is very cute. I guess I worry about younger women getting his attention."

Nanette let out a sigh. "Yeah. I get that. A lot of our customers come here for treatment because they want the same thing as you - the admiration of others. Be it a romantic partner, co-workers, friends, or even family members. But you don't need that," she whispered.

Damn it to hell, I thought to myself. I had to find the one ethical dental hygienist in the office. I needed more time there so that I could see Edna Nazario, and then somehow ascertain that she was the right one.

Nanette was about to say something else when a scrubs-clad woman came in, holding a clipboard. She whispered something to Nanette and then gave me a half-smile before leaving the office.

But it was enough. The scrubs-clad woman's nametag read 'Edna.'

Chapter Nineteen

"Marta? We notice that you left your social security number off the application," Nanette said.

"That's right," I said.

"We need that for billing," Nanette said.

I shook my head. "You don't. I am not paying with insurance - and even if I was, I have an insurance number independent of my social, so you don't need that."

Nanette's face tightened up. "Well, we can't do business then."

I nodded. "I understand. I appreciate your telling me that I don't need a tooth bleaching."

"Well, no one needs it," she said, backpedaling a bit. "Maybe it would benefit you."

I stared at her for a second. I got the feeling that her soft approach was giving way to a harder one. Just then, the woman named Edna entered the office again.

"You know, this consult, while free, costs us money," she said. "It is time Nanette provided that could have gone to a paying customer."

I took a second to stare at Edna. She was Puerto Rican looking for sure. Her eyes were slightly slanted, and she had the heart-shaped face I'd seen frequently back on the island. I noticed that she didn't wear much jewelry and that her make-up was muted. Her peach shoes looked decidedly expensive.

"And yes, we have the right to ask for your social security number," Edna added.

"I am sure that your management tells you to ask for that. However, citizens are only required to give their social security numbers to their employers, banking institutions, real estate closing companies, health insurance companies, and credit card companies. So, while you can request my social, I am not obligated to give that to you."

I watched as Edna looked down at the clipboard. "I notice that you didn't list your place of business."

"I didn't," I said.

Nanette's demeanor changed. She shook her foot and twisted a ring on her finger while forcing a smile my way. Nanette was nervous. Edna, however, was as cool as a cucumber.

"I think we're done here, Miss Morales," she sharply said.

I smiled at her. "What part of Arecibo are your people from?" I asked of her.

Her eyes widened quickly. She stiffened and dropped the pen that had been sitting on the clipboard.

"How do you know about Arecibo?" Edna asked as she picked up the pen from the floor.

"My people are from there. It was only our grandparents' generation that began to migrate from Puerto Rico to the United States. Before that, they stuck to their pueblos, and barrios, and sectors. Even after they moved stateside, Puerto Ricans usually married the people that were familiar to them - fellow Puerto Ricans. That's why you see the same features in our people - almond eyes and heart-shaped faces in pretty women like you." I said to her as I smiled.

Edna nodded a few times. "Well...as intriguing as that is, our business is done here. Thank you for coming, Miss Morales. We'll find you if we need more information from you."

I stood up and grabbed my purse. "You can try," I said to Edna as I smiled.

Nanette looked pale as I turned to her. "Thank you for your expertise, Nanette."

Heart pumping, I dashed out of the office and made it to my car. Once there, I pulled out of the lot and parked down the road at a Panera Bread.

From the comfort of my car, I made a call.

"Marta?" inquired Doña Elena.

"Hi, Doña Elena. How are you?"

"I am well. Do you have information for me?"

Straight to the point, she was. "I do. I've done my work. I found Edna Nazario."

I heard her sudden intake of breath. "Did you see her?"

"Even better. I spoke to Edna."

"Oh, my goodness. Goodness. Let me sit down."

Feeling slightly alarmed, I patiently waited for Doña Elena to come back on the line.

"Okay. Okay. Tell me...what does Edna look like?"

For a moment, I thought about how to describe Edna to Doña Elena. "Edna Nazario looks like she walked out of a house in the hills of Esperanza. She is Puerto Rican. She's who you are looking for."

"Wow. Wow. Did you take Edna's picture?"

I groaned. "I did not. You did not request that."

"How many hours workhours do you have left in the deposit?"

"About six hours," I said.

"How is that possible?"

"My going rate is thirty dollars an hour. Not only that, but money for expenses is deducted from that deposit. That leaves six hours."

Doña Elena let out a breath. "Fine. Six hours."

"Unless I have to do other work from home."

"Fine!" she snapped.

I forced myself to take a calming breath. "Alright, Doña Elena. Let's reset expectations here. You wanted me to find Edna Nazario for you, and I did that. You have a handful of hours left. What else do you want?"

"I want pictures of Edna Nazario. I want to know where she lives. I want pictures of her place of business."

I let out a breath. "Okay. I will get those. Would you like to know my opinion about Edna?"

"Of course I do," she said.

"Okay. I can give you something quickly now. I will generate something longer and a bit more detailed later. I will have that delivered to you in Puerto Rico."

"What is she like?"

I thought of my impression of Edna. "I think she's a sketchy character, Doña Elena."

"Good," Doña Elena said on a sigh. "That's good to know."

I disconnected with Doña Elena. I grabbed my tape recorder and talked about what went down during my visit to Visions of Teeth. I would transcribe it to paper later.

Twenty minutes later held me looking at my cell phone. It was near lunchtime, and I still had cleaning jobs to get to. I turned my car on and headed out.

Scrubbing Jane's shower walls, I formulated a plan for my evening. I would finish Jane's condo, would hit up the pawnshop, and would go home to change and then stake out Visions of Teeth. They closed the shop at eight p.m., so I figured I had time.

I rinsed the shower and then quickly mopped the bathroom floor. I was in the kitchen and about to leave when Jane Knight stopped me.

"Marta," she said.

I turned to her. "Yeah, Jane?"

She stared out the window for a moment, looking like she was trying to focus. She shook herself and smiled at me.

"Nevermind, Marta. You have other stuff to get to."

I did. Still, I sat my bag down on Jane's table.

"I have nothing else better to do tonight."

Jane stared at me, suddenly looking nervous. Her nerves made me nervous. Thinking quickly, I walked to her fridge and opened it. There, I saw the cooked pot roast.

"Do you want me to make you some roast sandwiches?"

She hugged her arms. "Yeah. Sure. Will you have one with me?"

"Hell, yes," I said as I pulled the roast and other ingredients out.

I pulled the skillet out from her oven and set it atop the cooktop. I buttered rustic bread and began to make the sandwiches.

"I have a crockpot. I make roasts about twice a month or so," I said as I didn't look directly at Jane. "I think it's a southern recipe? Not Puerto Rican. I used to just eat the seasoned meat with baked potatoes on the side. Maybe some steamed broccoli, too. But then one day, I decided to change something just a little bit. Just to try it out," I said as I glanced back at her.

Jane was sitting on the barstool and stared at me. I carried on.

"So, I decided to make sandwiches out of them. It was a revelation for me, how good they were. Which is kind of funny," I said as I laughed. "Other folks probably cook them this way all the time."

Once I'd prepared Jane's sandwich, I set it on a plate and presented it to her. I plated my own and sat next to her at the bar. I had a few bites of my sandwich.

From the corner of my eye, I noticed Jane crying as she ate her sandwich.

"You are a strong, strong woman, Jane. So fierce," I gently said. Still, I looked at my roast and not at her. "I think that maybe you are taking pills to...change your mood?"

Her head whipped my way. "What did you see?"

I shook my head as I looked at her. "Nothing. Save for your behavior differences. It's not my business," I said as I set my sandwich down. "I...just want you to know that I think you are amazing - just as you are. I think that women would want to take pills to be like you when you are not on pills."

Jane started sobbing. She got up and set her sandwich on her plate before dashing into the hallway.

"Please. Enjoy your sandwich. It's good. You can clean the kitchen tomorrow. I'm tucking in," she said. She then ran towards the stairs and her room, I presumed.

I let out a breath and gathered her plate and my own. I set them in the sink and then made my way out of her condo. In my car, I looked at my clock. I'd only spent about fifteen more minutes at Jane's than I'd planned. I hoped that time helped her.

Jamie's Pawnshop was closed for business but open for me. Jamie was there, working some books.

"Marta! How are you?" he asked.

I smiled at him. "Good. Staying busy. How are things?"

He let out a breath. "Good. Thank God. Well, sort of."

I stopped walking to the cleaning closet and stared at him. The 65-year-old looked at me for a minute. "My daughter. She keeps crap books. I have to come in and make sure she's doing everything right."

I nodded. "Can you hire that out?"

Jamie groaned. "If only. But I can't. I'm morally obligated to employ my daughter. My wife would kill me if I suggested otherwise."

"Does she like the work?"

Jamie appeared to think about it. "She loves being around family. She likes customers. That's worth something. But, she likes fashion and makeup. Not pawnshop retail," he said as he motioned the store.

For a moment, I wondered what Hector would be doing, had he lived. Accounting? Would he be cleaning with me, or passed out on my couch or Waleska's?

"It's a work in progress - raising kids. It isn't done when they leave home. It definitely isn't done for me, as my daughter still lives at home. It's the Greek way. But not the American way."

I nodded. "For Puerto Ricans - the traditional ones still on the island - the couple moves out as soon as they marry."

"Did you?"

I nodded. "I did. Did you?"

He shook his head. "No. My wife and I lived with my family for about a year or so after we married. It was good, but sometimes chafing. It was after Vietnam, though. It was good to have family close."

I stared off again, and Jamie laughed. "I am going to stop talking to you about kids and wars. There are other things to talk about," he added. "Such as kids that can't do basic math."

I laughed out loud. "Agreed. I have a bookkeeper that helps keep me on track."

"Do you now? Is she any good?"

I shrugged. "Well, Ada's services are free but good. But I think she's a gossip."

Jamie laughed out loud. "You get what you pay for."

"Isn't that the truth." I shook my head, remembering what I was supposed to be doing. "With that in mind, let me get to minding my business by cleaning yours."

"You're a professional," he said.

"As are you," I said.

I made my way to the cleaning closet and carried on. Before leaving, I spoke to him one more time.

"Jamie?"

"Yeah, Marta?"

"Your friend...Barney's Haberdashery, does he still need a maid?"

"I can check. Thinking about expanding?"

I shrugged. "I might have a client who will need to move on, so maybe."

"I'll have an answer for you next week."

"Thank you, Jamie."

"Of course."

Chapter Twenty

I dashed home and quickly changed my clothing. I dressed in dark pants, a dark shirt, and a dark jacket. After, I ran to my car and headed to Visions of Teeth.

As predicted, the office was still open. I parked across the street from them and climbed into my backseat. I found that my slightly dimmed passenger windows did an excellent job of hiding me. Also, folks tended to look at front seats before they looked at backseats.

My cell phone chose that moment to ring, and I groaned as I looked at the Caller ID. It was Melissa. I wanted to talk to her, but I couldn't. I rejected the call and made a mental note to call her later. Keeping my camera close, I kept looking at Visions of Teeth.

Finally, Edna Nazario and Mayra walked out of the front doors. I zoomed in on them and took as many pictures as I could. For some reason, I decided to take photos of their vehicles and their license plates. Being that I was already there, I took pictures of the rest of the employees as they left.

Once every single car had left the Visions of Teeth parking lot, I turned on my car, which coincided with my phone ringing again. I put it on speaker and answered it.

"Hello?"

"Hey. What are you up to?" asked Kevin.

I bit my lip as I considered it. "Just coming home from a late job."

"It's almost nine o'clock. Who do you clean for that late?"

I let out a breath. "If I have more things going on during the day - personal appointments and whatnot - some of my clients are okay with me coming in later in the evening."

"Did you have a personal appointment today?"

"What's with all the questions?"

"Because I'm curious. Because I care," Kevin said.

"I had a dental appointment this morning. I ran late with another client, which shifted everything else on my schedule. But I'm on my way home now. What have you been up to today?"

"Work stuff. Detective stuff. Cop stuff."

"No. I'm going to need more than that, Detective Connelly."

"Why?" he said as he let out a breath.

"You just asked me very pointed questions. I have the right to ask the same. But I'm not," I said as I turned down a road. "I just want more than what you've given."

"Fine. Okay. A drug bust went down. A spoke with an informant today. I had to skip lunch, which is why I am calling you now. Do you want to get dinner?"

I smiled. "That's a yes."

I met him at a small deli about ten minutes away from my place.

"Tell me about your day," Kevin said as he had a drink of his beer.

I thought about what I could tell him. "I talked to my pawnshop client about raising kids - adult ones - and how hard it is. Again, I wondered what Hector would be into, should he have survived the war. Jamie told me about his daughter and how she isn't the best employee, but how he couldn't do anything about it."

Kevin laughed. "Good old nepotism."

"Tell me about your parents," I said to him.

"Dad's a doctor, and mom's a lawyer."

Kevin's parents' occupations had come up in conversation before. I was impressed and intimidated over their professions, and I was also not in a hurry to meet them.

"They still okay with you being a cop?"

"I don't know. It's been nearly twenty years now, so they're used to it."

Looking at Kevin, I wondered who the ginger was - his mother or his father. I thought to ask but then worried about him talking about meeting parents. Was my assumption premature? Perhaps. I took a risk.

"Who's the ginger? Your mom or your dad?"

He bit into a fry. "Both. Kind of," he qualified with a shake of his head. "Mom's ginger. Dad's blond, but his father is red-headed."

I nodded.

"You're okay with gingers," he said.

I laughed. "Well, one in particular."

He laughed out loud. "Good to know."

I sipped my beer before speaking again. "I know that some people have hang-ups with gingers, but I don't get it." I stared at how his hair went from red to orange and gold. "It looks like fire, or like a sunset. It's so alive. So vibrant."

Kevin stared at me as if his life depended on it. I continued speaking. "Most folks in Puerto Rico are brunettes. Lots of Spaniards - most, I think - have dark hair. Then there's the Native American Taino DNA, and then African DNA. Of course, other groups immigrated. There are gingers on the island and natural blonds, too. But mostly brunettes, which is fine. The darker complexion helps with the constant sun."

Kevin nodded and sat back. "You've got it for me, bad, Marta," he said.

I laughed out loud. "Do I?"

"Yes. You love redheads, and you are down with what I've got."

Kevin laughed while I rolled my eyes.

"Well, I like you, so there's that."

"For sure," he said.

108

I stifled a yawn.

"Goodness. My charm has expired," he said as he looked at his wristwatch.

"I'm just tired. It's been a long day. Got an early day tomorrow, too."

"Let me walk you to your car."

Kevin settled the tab and escorted me to my vehicle.

"Kevin?"

"Yeah."

"I think I want to know - formally - where the case is with Maria Alvarez. How can I go about doing that?"

He let out a breath. "You can come to the station tomorrow. What's your schedule looking like?"

We agreed on a time. Kevin opened the door to my vehicle but didn't release the handle or allow me in. He bent his head to mine and kissed me.

"Tongue kisses are coming soon," he warned.

I laughed. "Maybe."

"Go home," he said as he finally opened the door. "Text me when you get there."

"Will do. Good night, detective."

He snuck another kiss and then stepped to the sidewalk. I felt safe and cherished. It was nice.

Once home, I imported the pictures from my digital camera to my laptop. I cropped some and deleted others. Having found enough good images of Edna Nazario, I attached those to an email to Doña Elena. I composed an email detailing all of the work I'd done for her. I was about to send it when I decided to see if my DNA results were in.

I logged into the website and found that they were. Delighted, I discovered my maternal haplogroup - A2 - my earliest maternal ancestress was Native American, which was not surprising. My DNA was mostly Spanish, with some Native American and African thrown in. I found a smattering of French and Italian as well. What surprised me was the number of people I was related to - it was over nine-hundred. Thinking quickly, I looked up Doña Elena and saw that she was my fourth cousin.

I decided to check if Edna Nazario was related to me. I found that she was a fourth cousin as well, but interestingly enough, Edna was not related to Doña Elena. Stunned, I stood up. I took a couple of steps back and looked at the laptop screen again.

Doña Elena was not related to Edna Nazario. Edna Nazario was not Doña Elena's niece. Doña Elena had hired me under false pretenses.

I grabbed my cell phone and called the home of my parents.

"Hi Mama," Dad said.

I let out a breath of relief. I was glad that I didn't have to go through my mom to get to him.

"Hey, Dad. How are you?"

"Good. Watching the *Capitanes* beat the *Piratas*." The *Capitanes* were the basketball team from Arecibo, and were very, very good - the best on the island.

"Sounds cool, Dad. Um. Can I pick your brain about something?"

I heard the sound of wood creaking and springs moving; I could picture my father raising himself from his recliner.

"Sure."

"Is mom within earshot?"

"How about I take you to the patio?"

I smiled. "That sounds great, Dad."

"Esteban? Where are you going?" asked Mom.

"To the *marquesina* to talk to my daughter."

"About what?"

"None of your business, woman."

My mom liked to harangue my dad. Thankfully, my mild-mannered father could give as good as he got. I heard the sliding glass door close.

"Aha," he said.

I sighed. "I am pretty sure that Doña Elena hired me under pretenses." I then explained what I'd found with the DNA tests, as well as the information I'd found for Doña Elena.

"Hmmm. I told you to question Doña Elena's motives, didn't I?"

Dad sounded a bit pissy.

I sighed. "Not in so many words, but yes, you did."

"Doña Elena didn't sign a contract with you. She doesn't have to be honest with you. She paid you for a service which you conducted. Now, you must deliver what you've promised."

I groaned. "Dad. But...what if she does something terrible with the information I've procured for her?"

"That's what contracts are for," he loudly said. "Liability."

I groaned. "I know, Dad."

"Here's what you do. You find out why Doña Elena wants that information. If you find that she's trying to do illegal things with the information, you return her deposit. There's no contract, so you are protected, too."

I let out a breath. "Could you brainstorm with me a bit?" I asked of him.

He laughed. "I'd like nothing better."

I went back to my laptop. "Dad, I am related to Edna Nazario. Edna has a small family tree on the website, and I know ours. If her tree is right and mine is, too, that means that we are related through you."

"How many generations?"

"Three to four," I said.

"Jesus Christ," he grumbled.

"Watch your mouth!" I heard mom yell.

So, she'd been eavesdropping. Not surprising and not unlike her. Dad ignored her.

"Do I need to tell you how many first cousins you have?" Dad asked me.

I groaned. "My first cousins number over fifteen on your side."

"That's just you," Dad tiredly said. "I have over seventy-five first cousins. First cousins! I can't even tell you how many second cousins and third cousins I have. The third cousin link you have might mean something with smaller families, but not from big, Catholic, farming families like ours. It means shit," Dad said.

"Watch your language!" Mom yelled.

"¡Callate la boca! ¡Estoy hablando!" Dad yelled back.

Crap. Dad was kind of pissy.

"Dad, if you're mad, I can handle this on my own."

"No. No. You called me, so we will handle it," Dad angrily said. "But you need to start thinking about who you go into business with! You need to think about protecting yourself. Because if things go bad, it is going to bite you in the ass, Marta Morales!"

"Okay, Dad. I'm sorry."

"Yeah, I know. Again, we need to discard the DNA connection between you and Edna Nazario, because it's a distraction. It is not going to tell you why Doña Elena wanted Edna Nazario found. Give me a second and let me think," he said as he sighed.

"Okay, Daddy."

"Aha. Can you see the names of the people that Edna is related to?"

I clicked around Edna's public profile. "Yeah. I can."

"Okay. Start giving me names. Starting with those that are closely related to Edna."

I found one that stuck out. "Dad. Javier Nuñez. He matches her by 25%! That means that he must be..."

"Her uncle," Dad volunteered. "Go back to her tree. See who you can find that has the last name Nuñez."

I did. "No one, Dad. It doesn't show up on her tree."

"Who is her father?"

"Charlie Daniels."

Dad scoffed. "Not likely. You said you saw her in person, right? Did she look half-white? Or half-black?"

I let out a breath. "We can't tell with everyone, I know. But if I had to guess, I'd say no. Edna looks like someone you'd see outside of mass in Esperanza."

"Who does the name 'Nazario' belong to?"

"Her mother."

"Okay. We are getting a picture here, now. Charlie Daniels was Edna Nazario's stepfather. Javier Nuñez is her uncle, but doesn't show up on her mother's side of the tree."

"Javier Nuñez is her paternal uncle?" I volunteered.

"Yes," Dad said. "Is he alive?"

I did some research and found that he was not. "No. Died two years ago."

"That's the strongest trail, Marta - Edna Nazario's paternal line. Go back to Doña Elena's tree."

I did. My mouth dropped open at what I saw. "Wow."

"What?" Dad barked.

"Doña Elena's second husband. His last name was Nuñez. Carlos Nuñez. But they didn't have any kids together. Doña Elena doesn't have any children of her own."

I got up and began to pace. "Do you think Edna knows who her father was?"

"I have no idea," Dad said. "But you need to leave that girl alone."

I nodded. "I agree. Something fishy about that one."

"All you were hired to do was find her. You did that."

"Okay, okay," I said as I let out a breath. "Do you think Doña Elena is going to do anything untoward with the information?"

"Doña Elena is a wealthy woman who got most of her money from her second husband. If it's found out that he had a kid, well, that kid might have a case to get some of that money."

"Shit, Dad," I said as I sank onto a chair.

"Look. It's time to bring your brother in on this."

"Okay," I said.

Moments later, my father had conferenced called my brother into the call.

"This had better be good," Rafy said. "Because it is eleven p.m., and I am fucking tired."

Quickly, I outlined everything I had found about Edna Nazario, Doña Elena, Doña Elena's deceased ex-husband, and his possible relation to Edna Nazario.

"Fuck," Rafy cussed.

"The most important thing here is your sister's protection," Dad said.

"Yeah, yeah. I know. Email me a picture of Edna."

"I can text that to you right now."

"Do it," Rafy said.

"Text it to me to my phone," Dad said.

Minutes later, both my brother and my father received Edna's picture.

"You are right," Rafy said. "She looks like. Like from the mountains, local," Rafy said.

"Zoraida!" Dad yelled into the phone.

"Dad!" I said as I rubbed my ear.

"Goodness, Papi," my brother complained.

"Where's my other cell phone?" Dad yelled.

"I've got it right here," Mom said. "Who is this girl in the picture?" she angrily asked.

"How did you unlock my phone?!" Dad barked.

"You never change your password! And what do you care? You have nothing to hide."

"Dear God, it feels like I'm back home," I muttered.

"Same," Rafy said as he groaned.

Dad was quiet for a moment. "She looks familiar," Dad said.

"You know who she looks like?" I overheard Mom say.

"Who?" Both Rafy and I asked, not that she could hear us.

"She looks like Claudia Nuñez. She works at the Humberto Vidal shoe store at the mall."

"Who's her father?"

"Javier Nuñez! Oh! You want to know who he is?" Mom loudly said.

"Carlos Nuñez' brother," I said.

Dad said the same thing out loud.

"How did you know that?" Mom said.

"Dad, please thank Mom," I implored. "If Mom had not given us that confirmation, who knows how far behind we'd be?"

Dad groaned. "Thank you, Zory," he said to my mom.

"You are welcome," she said.

I heard the glass door open and close and knew that my dad had gone to the marquesina again.

"Here's what you do, Marta; you fulfill your contract with Doña Elena. BUT, you only do that as soon as your brother is outside of her house."

"That sounds good, Dad," Rafy said. "I got time tomorrow evening."

"Works for me," I said.

"Okay, kids. You did good work."

"You did most of it, Dad," I said.

Dad chuckled.

"*You did most of it, Dad,*" my brother parroted.

"This was fun, Marta. But you need to think about contracts in the future," my father advised.

"I will."

"Okay. I'll call you tomorrow," Rafy said to me. He let out a breath. "And thank you for the heads-up. If I can prevent someone from hurting someone else, it's a good day. Heck, I'll tell some other guys in the station, just in case."

"And remember that you are not obligated to tell Doña Elena what you've learned about Edna Nazario. But wait a minute. Shit. Your name and DNA are on the website," Dad protested. "Doña Elena is going to know."

"Fuck," Rafy cussed. "Dad's right."

I smiled. "No. I used a pseudonym."

I could hear my dad's laughter. "Good girl."

"But your email. Is it attached to your DNA profile?" Rafy asked.

"No. I got a dummy email address. This isn't my first day, you know," I said.

It was midnight by the time I got off the phone. Still, I took the time to make a ton of notes regarding what I'd discovered about Edna Nazario's relation to Doña Elena's second husband. I even prepared the ones I would present to Doña Elena.

My mind and body exhausted, I happily gave in to sleep.

Chapter Twenty-One

I had a busy, busy day, so I got up nice and early for it. After I had a quick breakfast, I headed to Jane Knight's condo. After parking outside her garage, I headed up the back steps and made a mental list of everything I had to do. The list was comprised of:
- Clean Jane's Condo
- Make it Erickson Ventures Chicago and apologize to Melissa for not calling her back (and schedule a bar meetup)
- Meet Kevin at the precinct
- Clean the two residential properties
- Meet with Ada to discuss my business expenses
- Standby for Rafy's call so that I can call Doña Elena with the updates.

There would be things in between, of course - things that might delay my schedule. Using my key, I let myself in Jane's place. She wasn't there, but Tim was. I stopped for a second as I watched him seated at the bar.

"Hello, Marta," he said.

"Good morning, Tim. How are you?" I asked as I hung my coat up in the coat closet, which was in the hall just off the kitchen.

"I don't know, Marta. But I have a question for you."

Nervously, I turned to him. Tim was a good-looking man. He had dark curly hair and big brown eyes. I knew that he had dimples when he smiled. They probably suited him well with his position at the district attorney's office.

"What's that, Tim?"

"I want to poach you, Marta. Jane and I will be taking a little break."

Wow. I stared at Tim, mentally willing him to say more.

"I've been spending a lot of time at work. I'll be renting a place in town. Will you be my maid?"

My eyes widened a bit. "I am flattered, Tim. Thank you. I am sure you would be a great boss. But Jane's my client. Kind of my boss."

Tim half-smiled. "I understand. You are loyal to her. Thank you for that."

I nodded. "Jane's great."

Tim's chin shook a bit. "Jane is. She's great just the way she is." Tim cleared his throat and then stood up. "Can you do me a favor?"

"What?"

"Keep an eye on her. Because Jane trusts you; therefore, I trust you. You see, we had a maid before we hired you. But Jane said that she heard you talking in the elevator, holding your own while arguing with a yuppie business executive. Jane thought that you would be someone good to know."

Tim's words surprised me. Tears filled my eyes, and I nodded.

"Jane's a great person to know, Tim. I promise I'll keep an eye out for her."

"Thank you. And maybe if Jane needs someone, you can call me?"

"It's not for me to reveal her confidences, Tim."

"I know; I mean if she gets hurt or something."

I nodded. "Okay. Sure."

"Thanks, Marta. Take care of yourself."

"You too, Tim."

With that, he grabbed his wallet and keys and headed out of the condo. The tears I'd been holding back fell from my eyes. My hand went to my mouth, and I let out a sob. Dear God. Had I encouraged Jane to break up with her husband?

I didn't have time for the breakdown. Also, Tim and Jane were the only people entitled to tears. I wiped my face and carried on with my cleaning. Already worried about Jane, I looked at her freezer and her fridge.

I was surprised when I saw an uncooked pot roast in her fridge. I looked through her cupboards and saw ranch dressing packets and pepperoncini peppers. Thinking quick, I called her.

"Yes, Marta," she said. Her voice sounded a bit ravaged.

"Yeah, hi, Jane. I'm at your place. I was sorting out the fridge when I saw your pot roast. Do you want me to put that in a crockpot for you? I can put it on low. It'll be perfectly cooked when you get home."

Hearing her sobs on the phone made me cuss myself.

"Jane? You sound busy," I deflected. "Nevermind–"

Jane cleared her throat. "Well, you might as well," she said, command restored to her tone. "You'll have one less person to clean for anyway. I pay you enough as is."

"Okay. I'll put the pot roast on for you."

"If that's all, I have work to do."

"Yes. Sure. Okay. Bye, Jane."

Using time I didn't have, I quickly threw the pot roast together. Jane would come home to a clean but empty condo tonight, and that would hurt. Perhaps a warm dinner would help with the sadness.

With the safety net that was Kevin's position, I sped to Erickson and Associates. Fifteen minutes late, I opened the doors and dashed in.

"Amiga! You are busting in her like the cops," Melissa said from her desk.

I was panting. Thankfully, Melissa was amused.

"Can't wait...to catch up...gotta clean first."

"Okay. I'll be here."

I dashed to the cleaning closet and then proceeded to clean Melissa's office, followed by her bathroom. I knocked on Niels' office door after.

"Good Morning, Marta," Niels said.

"Good Morning, Mr. Ericskon," was my reply. "Would you prefer me to clean your bathroom first this morning?"

"Please do," he said.

"Yes, Sir."

I didn't have time for Niels' crazy. I quickly - but expertly - cleaned his bathroom. After, I made it to his office. He grabbed his cell phone and got up from his desk.

"I won't be long," I said to him.

"Take your time, Marta. I have time."

Not humoring him, I turned the vacuum on proceeded to clean his carpet. I dusted after, happily noticing that he was gone. I ran the vacuum again and then gathered all of the office trash.

"You are a hurricane this morning," Melissa said to me as she stood up from her desk.

I nodded. "I have such a busy day, and it isn't even halfway over."

I set the trash bags down and pulled my cell phone out. "Okay. I am looking at my calendar. What works for you for a bar meetup?"

Melissa smiled and pulled her own phone out. "Friday night?"

I cringed. "I have a date that night. How about Sunday evening?"

"That works!" she said. "Same place?"

"At six? I'll be there."

She laughed. "Okay. But you still have to call me to catch up!"

"I will! Take care!" I said as I grabbed the trash and left.

After depositing Erickson's trash in a large chute located by the service elevators, I went to the garage and called Kevin.

"Yeah. Can you be here in fifteen? I am slammed today," he said.

I looked at my clock. "Can you get me out of a speeding ticket?"

Kevin groaned. "God. Fine. But get here and don't get in an accident!"

"Roger that, Detective."

So, I dashed to the station. I was fatigued by the time I made it to Kevin's floor. I was nervous as I approached the desk secretary.

"Hi. I'm Marta Morales. I'm here to see Detective-"

Just then, a handsome, shave-headed, muscular detective came my way. "I've got this, Shirley," Detective James Kostas vibrato carried.

I smiled at him. I probably blushed, too. "Hello, James. How are you?"

"I'm good. It's been a while," James said as he took a step back. "I was expecting to hear from you after your Puerto Rico vacation."

Nervously, I clutched at my purse handles. "I've been busy. Plus, I didn't want to bother you. You said you'd call me with Maria Alvarez updates, and I know you have other things on your plate."

"You are never a bother," he said.

"Thank you."

A vibrating song came from James' belt. "Alright. Connelly's on his way. He's been nagging me about Maria updates."

"He's diligent."

"That he is. Let's go to a room to talk."

James escorted me to a conference room. "Marta? I've got a trainee detective. Do you mind if he sits in on this?"

I shook my head. "No. Of course not. The more heads, the better."

"Clever lady you are," he said before stepping away.

Too nervous to sit down, I paced the small space. I looked out the window to the door and looked for Kevin. Moments later, James stepped in with a detective in tow that I did not know.

"Hello, Miss Morales. I am Detective Walsh," said the tall black man.

I reached for his hand. "It is nice to meet you, Detective."

"Let's get started, Marta," said James.

I looked around. "Detective Connelly?"

"Talking with the Captain regarding another case. He'll be here momentarily."

I felt unease fill me. What was my old boss, Maria Alvarez, getting into? Did she put a hit on me? Where was Kevin?

I thought that going to the precinct to see Kevin would be different and fun. I was so nervous.

"You okay?" asked Detective Kostas.

I shrugged. "I don't know. I know that I need to know what Maria's getting into, so, here I am. But I am nervous."

Just then, Kevin walked in. I let out a breath of relief and sat down.

"Hey, you okay?" he asked of me.

Tears filled my eyes. "I don't know. I don't know why I'm scared."

Kevin sat next to me and gently held my face. "I would have told you if you had anything to worry about, okay?"

I swallowed. "Okay. Yeah."

Kevin smiled at me. "It's nice seeing you in the middle of the day."

I nodded. Detective Kostas cleared his throat. "If we can get started," he requested.

"Go for it," Kevin said.

Detective Kostas let out a breath. "I don't know where Maria Alvarez is. She disappeared after she got into your car. We lifted her prints from your backseat, but that didn't give us anything to work with."

I sat back in my seat. "At all? You don't know where she is...at all?"

118

Detective Kostas and Walsh shook their heads. "No. But we are keeping an eye out."

Bewildered, I shook my head. "Have you guys tried calling police officers in Puerto Rico? Seeking out her family members in Ponce?"

"Her crimes aren't big enough for us to go out there looking for her," James gently explained.

"She tried to KILL me, and that isn't a big enough reason?" I loudly asked. "She used my name to take money from a large law firm! Maria Alvarez is a low-level street thug, and you have nothing?"

Detective Kostas' nostrils flared, and he let out a breath. Even Detective Walsh looked put out with me.

"This is Chicago, Marta. We are busy. We have people getting killed left and right," James said.

"Okay. Then why don't you just go ahead and add me to that number!" I said as I stood up.

Kevin stood up and put his hands on my arms. "I'm sorry, Marta. I told you they didn't have anything," he implored.

"This sucks, Kevin!" I said as tears filled my eyes. "At this point, I could do a better job of finding Maria. Maybe that's what I have to do to stay safe."

"Don't do that," James said from his side of the table.

I was done listening to him, though. I was no longer a priority, which I could understand. Terror filled me anew.

"Hey. Hey," Kevin said as he wiped tears from my face. "You think I'm going to let anyone hurt you?"

"You can't be everywhere all the time," I said as I wiped my face. "You can't."

"I will do what I have to," he said.

"That's not your job," I whispered to him.

"Then what is?" he asked.

I let out a breath. "You're just my boyfriend," I whispered.

Kevin beamed. "Finally. Can we be Facebook official now?"

I laughed, and he did, too. Kevin hugged me. It felt so good.

"Um. Is something else going on here?" Detective Kostas asked.

Shyly, I detached from Kevin's embrace. Kevin kept his arm around me, though.

"Yeah. Marta's my girlfriend."

Detective Kostas nodded very slowly. "Oh. Really?"

"Yeah," Kevin said.

"You didn't say anything," James sniped.

"I didn't have to," Kevin replied.

"You can't be on this case and date the victim!" James angrily said.

"That's why I got off the case a month ago," Kevin calmly replied.

"Is this true, Marta?" James asked me.

I nodded. "Yes. But that isn't relevant to this case. I thought you knew where Maria was. But you don't. I have to look out for myself now. Again."

Even Kevin let out a breath. "Marta? James is busy. He checks in on Maria's contacts. So does Detective Walsh."

"If I may?" asked the tall detective.

I looked his way.

"I've been reading up on your case, Miss Morales," said Detective Walsh. "I know Maria's details well. Who her husband is, where her parents live, and where her friends are. Maria Alvarez is a priority. She's doing a good job of hiding her tracks, but we will find her."

Would they found her before she would find me, though? Not wanting to give the polite detective a hard time, I looked at my watch. "I have more work to do, Kevin."

"I'll be by tonight," he said as he took a step closer to me.

"It'll be late."

"I'll be there," he asserted.

I looked at Detective Walsh and Detective Kostas, who looked a bit angry.

"Thank you, Detectives," I said. "I'll see myself out."

"I'll walk you," Kevin said.

He walked me to my vehicle but stopped me at my car door. "I am so sorry that we didn't have better news for you."

I blinked my tears away. "I should have known. I guess I was hoping for more."

"Maybe you should take off for the rest of the day," he suggested.

I shook my head. "No. I can't. And it's alright. Cleaning will distract me."

"I'll be over with donuts," he said before kissing me. He then laughed.

"What's funny?"

"You're my girlfriend."

I laughed. "I guess so."

"That means tongue," he said.

I shook my head. "That doesn't sound sexy - not when you put it like that."

"I'll put it another way," he whispered.

"I'm going now."

"You know where to find me," he said.

"I do."

With that, I departed. I rushed through the cleanings of both of my residential customers before heading to a local bakery to meet Ada.

When I arrived, she already had two steaming, chocolate chip cookies waiting for me along with a coffee.

"The cookies are hot," Ada quickly said. "I made sure that they didn't pour the coffee until about two minutes ago, so it should be scalding."

I stared her down as I removed my coat and sat it on an empty chair along with my purse.

"I am sorry," she said as I sat down.

"What are you sorry for?" I asked.

Ada let out a breath. "Anibal's wife - Gretchen - is on the board for a special needs school. My niece - Alondra - is highly autistic. My sister is a single mom and is doing all she can for Alondra. I thought that getting Alondra into the special school would help my niece and my sister."

Fuck. There went my anger.

"Did it help?"

Ada smiled. "Yes! Alondra is more verbal now. My sister gets respite time twice a month, now. They are happier, and I am happier."

"Did Gretchen's help come with strings?"

Ada's smile faded. "Yes. Gretchen said that I was to call her if Anibal were to...pursue you again."

I rolled my eyes. "For God's sake, Ada!" I exclaimed. "I am not going after him! I am the one who dumped him!"

Ada shook her head. "Gretchen is concerned about Anibal pursuing *you*," she said in a low voice. "I was obligated to call her and tell her that you were speaking to Anibal. If someone else told her before me, well, it might hurt Alondra's chances at the school."

"Is Gretchen that vicious?"

Ada shook her head again. "No, she isn't. But, we had an agreement - Gretchen, and I. Because she still worries about you."

"A woman who steals a married man kinda deserves that fear," I said.

Ada shrugged, and I sipped my coffee and winced. She was right; it was hot.

"How can I trust you not to rat out my financial stuff to Gretchen?"

Ada let out a breath. "I am sorry. You have every right to be concerned." She paused for a moment before speaking again. "I understand your fear, but I want you to know that I keep your finances private from everyone - even Anibal. I want you to do well, Marta. Because I think you are cool," she said, her voice cracking. "I am kind of invested now. I promise that I will give you my best."

Damn. That was a good speech.

"Okay," I said as I let out a breath. "But, please do me a favor."

"What?"

"Tell me first - if you feel that you have to share anything with Gretchen."

She nodded. "I will."

"I am going to eat my cookies now," I said as I gave her a bit of side-eye.

She laughed. "You'd better. Those cookies aren't cheap."

"But they're good," I said after having a bite of a cookie. "So much better than the stuff at-"

Ada smiled at me. "Panera. I know. Okay. Let's talk turkey."

It turned out to be a very productive meeting, thankfully. Ada was in my good graces again. Also, I came away with a better understanding of her, and even the *puta* Gretchen.

I thought about Anibal's women as I drove home. His employee, Ada, was a woman who valued family more than she did her work. I respected that. Gretchen *la puta* lived in fear of her husband Anibal's roving eye. That was a sucky way to live. I remember the way he'd talked to her on the phone, back when I was in his office talking about Waleska and Adan. Anibal was very sharp with Gretchen. Did that mean he didn't respect her?

I sighed for Gretchen. She'd landed herself a well-off, handsome husband. They had children together. But, she would also live in fear forever.

"That sucks," I said as I parked outside my apartment building.

I was glad that Gretchen had taken that problem off of my hands.

Chapter Twenty-Two

I had a long shower and put my sweats on. I had an easy dinner of ramen noodles. After that, I called my brother.

"Aha, aha. *Perate un momento*," Rafy said to me.

I stifled my groan and sank on the couch.

"I was driving," he explained. "It rained all day, and the roads are slick. These mountains in Esperanza are a bitch when they are wet."

I was glad I hadn't sniped at him.

"Should I call Dad?"

"Yeah. Conference call him real quick. I'm getting close to Doña Elena's property right now."

So, I conferenced called my dad, who'd been anxiously awaiting my call.

"Marta: you give her what she paid for - no more and no less. Email her ONLY the things you discussed with her—nothing else."

"Okay, Dad."

Rafy chimed in. "Alright. I see her car. I think she's in her living room. Go ahead and call her, Marta, on your other phone. Put it on speaker and mine and Dad's call on speaker. We'll mute our calls while we listen to your call."

"Okay," I replied.

After following Rafy's instructions, I called Doña Elena.

"Hello?" she said on the second ring.

"Hi, Doña Elena; this is Marta."

"I know it's you. I have caller ID, after all," she dryly said.

The Doña Elena I had gotten to know was not the same Doña Elena I'd first met. I'd have to pull at that thread later, though.

"I am about to send you an email right now. It contains all of the information I've ascertained on Edna Nazario."

"Why couldn't you send this two days ago?"

"Because I was assembling the report, Doña Elena."

"I just don't know why it took you this long."

"When we went into business, I told you that it would take six weeks to attain the information. It's been a month."

"Fine. Whatever. What do you have to tell me?"

I proceeded to provide Edna's full name, where she worked, where she lived (which I'd gotten from a website), what her schedule appeared to be, what car Edna drove, and what she looked like.

"That's basic information. I need more," Doña Elena said.

"That's what you paid for."

"I could have gotten that!" she protested.

I could think of at least four ways to tell Doña Elena to go to hell, but in the end, I was a professional.

"This concludes our contract, Doña Elena."

"What? That's it? I need more. I can pay for more," she quickly said.

"I don't have time in my schedule to devote to this pursuit, Doña Elena. I can give you the names of other private investigators, though."

"I can do that myself!"

I then heard a dial tone.

"Wow," I said as I hung up.

I then got on the phone with my dad and my brother. "Did you guys hear all of that?"

"Yeah. *Es una víbora*," Dad said.

"Yeah, and I am about to go to that snake's house," Rafy said. "I'm going to get off the phone. I'll call you back soon."

When it was just my dad and me on the phone, he spoke. "You did well by not accepting more money from her."

"That was an easy no," I said. "Doña Elena isn't who I thought she was, Dad. When I met her before, she was super nice."

"That could be one of three things. Doña Elena thought she could get your services free or on the cheap. When Doña Elena realized she couldn't push you around like she does the rest of her friends and acquaintances, she got pissy. Or, you simply got to know her better. Or, maybe she simply didn't like you."

"Ouch, Dad," I said. "I'm likable." I defended.

"In friendships or as a maid, probably. Friendliness is not for private investigators. When you are a private eye, you see people's secrets. And then they sometimes have to pay you even while they reveal those secrets."

I let out a breath and sank into my couch. "I hadn't considered that."

"Think about it; you get paid to do the tacky things your clients don't want to do. They think they are keeping their hands clean, but they aren't. You are a reminder of their dirty deeds."

"Ouch, Dad," I said again.

"This line of work is not for everyone, *hija*. But you are good at it."

A short time later, Rafy called both my Dad and me.

"Yeah?" I quickly said.

"Hold on, hold on," Rafy said. "I'm pulling into the Church's drive-through."

"Bring me a number #4," Dad said.

Rafy groaned. "I wasn't headed your way, Dad."

"But now you are. Hold on," Dad said. "*Zoraida! What do you want from Church's Chicken?*" Dad had hollered to mom.

"For God's sake," Rafy protested.

I chuckled.

"Lucky you, sitting in Chicago," Rafy said.

"Your mother wants a #4, too."

"I guess I want a #4, too," Rafy said.

I, too, could have gone for the chicken and mashed potatoes combo, I found.

Ten minutes later, Rafy spoke. "Okay. So, I went in there and politely reintroduced myself. Doña Elena then served me some coffee and donuts, which weren't bad at all. I then told her that the reason for my visit was to advise her of harassment laws in Puerto Rico and Chicago, as well. I told her about the FBI - but all in a friendly manner."

"How did she take it?" I asked.

"Doña Elena got so pale! She almost dropped her coffee cup!"

"Goodness," I said.

"That was shame and fear, Rafy," Dad said. "Doña Elena was going to act on the information your sister gave her."

Rafy let out a breath. "I know. I politely scared her straight. The local cops know about it now, though."

"Thank you, Rafy," I said. "And you, too, Dad. You masterminded this."

"Yes," Dad said. "But you and your brother were my good foot soldiers."

Rafy scoffed, and I laughed.

"Hey, before you go," Rafy said. "Why the hell did Doña Elena ask me about my flatulence problem?"

I sputtered and laughed. "Oh. You know what? I got another call," I said.

"Marta!" Rafy called.

"*Aha, aha. Perate un momento*," I said before hanging up with my brother and my father.

Chapter Twenty-Three

The next morning, I woke up feeling clear-headed. Ada and I were on the same page - personally speaking, and professional speaking. I had a lead on a new cleaning gig. I'd concluded my business with Doña Elena. I knew what was going on with Jane Knight. While my old boss' whereabouts were still unknown, I knew that my safety was not being ignored. Also, Kevin and I were now boyfriend-and-girlfriend. He'd reminded me of that when he came over last night with donuts. I might have let his kisses go a bit longer than usual.

I put some ambient music on my radio before climbing out of bed. I smiled as I stretched. I looked in the mirror and liked what I saw. My long, dark, wavy hair looked pretty good. My white nightgown made me look younger, too.

"Life is exciting again," I said to my reflection.

I got to work. Jane Knight wasn't home. In her refrigerator were the crock-pot fixings for chicken and vegetables, though. I groaned as I looked at the ingredients sitting next to each other on a shelf.

"If you keep this up, I am going to charge you for cooking services," I said out loud.

Still, I chopped the vegetables and placed them into the crockpot along with some seasonings. I set it on low and carried on with the rest of my cleaning. At Erickson and Associates, Melissa greeted me warmly.

"I cannot wait to have drinks," she said as she hugged. "But I have a conference call. We'll catch up later!"

"Sounds good!" I said.

I cleaned hers and Niels' offices before moving on to their bathrooms, the waiting area, and then departed. Jamie was at the pawnshop and had the contact information for his friend Barney.

"He's waiting for your call," Jamie said.

"I'll call him this evening."

My residential clients weren't home, which was great. I cleaned their houses quickly but thoroughly. That night I had another great date with Kevin. We held hands more and kissed more, too.

The following week held more of the same. I didn't actively pursue sleuthing jobs, as I felt like I was still untangling the mess that was the Doña Elena/Edna Nazario job. When it was all said and done, I was sure to complete a thorough after-action report. Still, the task felt unfinished.

I hung out with Melissa but went shopping instead of going drinking. Melissa was great fun, as she pointed out stores and labels and how they were doing financially. She even had ideas about what the struggling companies could do better.

"You could do this anywhere, couldn't you?" I asked of her.

Melissa had been looking at a jacket when I said that. She hung it up before turning to me.

"Can you keep a secret?"

I nodded. "Of course."

"I am going home. Back to P.A."

Tears filled my eyes. Still, I smiled.

"Why are you smiling?" Melissa asked, even as her voice trembled.

"I am going to miss you," I said. "But the thought of you at home with your family? Loving on you and supporting you? You building a small, happy life? That's the dream, and I want that dream for you."

"But won't you miss me?" she asked.

I nodded. "Yes. So much. But we women have starts and stops in life, and that's okay. That's the way we grow."

"I don't know how to tell Niels."

The thought of her boss/lover made my tears dry very quickly. "You just go, Melissa. You pack your shit, and you go," I said as I grabbed her arm. "Don't wait for a reference or permission. If you wait for his consent, he will make that move difficult or impossible."

Melissa let out a breath. "When did you know?"

"About what?"

Melissa rolled her eyes. "Don't play coy."

"Let's walk," I said.

We left the department store and walked into the mall.

"I think I learned that you were having an affair with Niels...probably as soon as it happened."

"Oh God," Melissa said.

I glanced at her and saw tears in her eyes.

"Hearing it out loud sounds horrible. I am not this person. I'm not."

I shrugged. "I don't believe you forced Niels into anything."

She scoffed. "No, I did not. Niels was compelling, and I was easily compelled."

Melissa confirmed that she and Niels had become lovers following Melissa's revelations that she had a stalker. Niels was there to dry her tears.

"You were vulnerable at the time."

"That's no excuse."

"If you are looking for someone to punish you, that's not going to be me."

We stopped at a vibrant window display. After staring at the crystal fruit pendants, she turned to me.

"Why do you think I have to...leave so abruptly?"

"Because Niels is a psychopath. You know that, right?"

Melissa shrugged and continued walking. "Kind of." She let out a breath. "Yeah, I know he is."

"Does he know where you are right now?"

She nodded. "Yes. Niels always knows what I am up to. He wasn't like that before we became lovers," she whispered.

"You are smart, good-looking, and hard-working. You will be able to rebuild. But you have to go," I said.

Melissa swallowed. "I don't know where to start."

"Do you love him?"

Melissa shook her head. "No. I think I am more dependent on him than anything else, which is so not how my mother raised me. Her parents came over from Cuba on boats. My mom's father - my maternal grandfather - was a drunk," Melissa confided. "My grandmother learned to make money and keep it secret. She taught my mother to do that, and my mom taught me."

"Do you have secret funds?"

Melissa smiled and nodded. "I do. I might not be as clever as Niels, but I have some tricks up my sleeve."

"Good."

"How would you do it?" Melissa asked me.

I smiled at the cherries and banana crystal earrings. "I would see it as an adventure or as a rebirth. I would get in my car and go," I said as I looked at her. "Today. Now."

"Surely it's not that urgent," she said.

My smile faded as I turned to her. "Melissa, Niels is onto the fact that I don't like him. I wouldn't be surprised if he questions you about this visit, or if he tries to tighten the yoke he has on you."

"Why do you think that?"

"When you were in P.A. and came back before you wanted? Niels asked if I was the one that told you to go on vacation. I said I was. He said he was going to call you back early."

Melissa's eyes widened. She suddenly began to walk again, and I joined her.

"Are you serious?"

I nodded. "I am."

"Why didn't you say anything?"

I shrugged. "I didn't know if you would have believed me. I was scared that it would have gotten back to Niels and if he would have...escalated."

"Damn. I went from a stalker to a psychopath," she said as she rubbed her arms.

We stopped by a restaurant/pub in the mall. "Let me buy you a drink," I said to Melissa.

"Okay."

When we were seated at the bar and drinking a couple of beers, I asked her a question.

"Melissa?"

"Yeah."

"Why did you go after a married man? Why did he cheat on his wife with you?"

Melissa groaned.

"I am not critical. I am not going to reprimand you. I just want to know."

"Fear and lust, on my part," she said as she stirred her drink. "Niels is so damned handsome. He is powerful, funny, and strong." Melissa looked at me before continuing. "He and his wife are on the outs, a bit - even before we started our affair. Niels wants to move back to Denmark, but she wants to stay here. It's been something they've been fighting over for years."

I groaned. "That'll do it."

"Yeah," Melissa said.

Her cell phone buzzed, then. "Fuck. It's him."

"Answer it," I said. "Make it seem like everything's fine. Don't lie about anything."

Melissa did as I advised.

"Hey, you," Melissa said. "No. I am still shopping. Marta and I are having a couple of drinks before shopping again. No, not tonight. We might catch a movie, but I'll call you tomorrow morning. Okay. Bye."

Melissa continued to stare at her phone. "I feel like he's watching me - tracking my movements. How do I get out of this?" she asked as she looked at me. "I need out - as soon as possible."

"I can help you."

"How?"

We went to Target. Using cash, Melissa bought a disposable cell phone. We found a quiet corner of the mall. Using her old cell phone, Melissa made a video. In the video, she stated her wishes and gave me verbal power of attorney.

We hugged each other outside the mall. Melissa cried as she hugged me. "Thank you. Thank you, friend."

"I will always be your friend," I said to her as I cried. "Go."

Weeping, she dashed to her car. I cried for a couple of minutes before going back into the mall and calling Kevin.

"Hey, girlfriend," he said to me as he laughed.

I swallowed tears and took a breath. "Will you help me?" I asked of him.

"What's going on?" he asked, all humor gone from his tone.

Twenty minutes later held him outside the mall doors. Once we were in his unmarked vehicle, I handed him Melissa's cell phone, where he watched the video.

"I, Melissa Graciela Del Rio Bollinger, authorize my friend, Marta Morales, to act as my power-of-attorney. I authorize her to go to my apartment to get my valuables and send them to me at my home in Pennsylvania," she said as her voice cracked. "I am leaving Chicago, Illinois, out of my own volition. I have entered into a dangerous affair with my married boss, Niels Erickson. For my safety, I feel that I have to leave that affair and my job in this abrupt manner. As we speak, I am driving away from Chicago and driving east to Pennsylvania. I can be reached at phone number 773-565-9525. Thank you."

Kevin turned off the phone. "Fuck. Fuck. Fuck," Kevin said.

"What? Did I advise her incorrectly?"

Kevin turned to me. "You advised her well. If all she has here in Chicago is you...and her dangerous lover, well, that's not much. Are you sure he's a psychopath?"

I nodded. "Yeah, Kevin. I am."

Kevin held the phone and nodded. "Melissa Bollinger is an adult. Clearly, not missing. Let's...go and abide by her wishes."

We went to Melissa's condo. Using a box she had in her closet, I packaged the important papers she held in a lockbox under her bed. I added personal mementos she'd requested as well. After that, we closed the box and headed to a shipping store. I overnighted the package to an address belonging to a paternal aunt of hers.

I cried as we drove away. Kevin, the sweet man that he was, pulled over and hugged me.

"Hey. You were a friend."

"But my friend's gone now," I said as I sobbed.

Kevin said no more. He kept staring at me as I dried my tears. "You know what? I was going to drive you home. But, my car's back at the precinct. I have a couple of things to tie up before I finish for the night. Do you want to come with me?"

I nodded. "Yes. Yes, please."

Kevin smiled. "Of course you do. You're a fool for me."

I laughed, happy that I was able to do so. I still had a hard time wrapping my mind around what Melissa had done. She'd left Chicago with the clothes on her back. With her car, as well.

"Do you think Niels' might be tracking her car?" I asked Kevin.

Kevin said nothing for a bit. "I don't know how...rational this all is, Marta. I get wanting to quit without giving two weeks' notice. But you have to tie up loose ends," he said as he tapped the steering well. "Melissa could have told her landlord. Is her boss slash lover this fearsome? To make her want to leave like this?"

"I think so."

Kevin shrugged. "Maybe. Maybe she was just looking for a reason to bail. Does she like Chicago?"

"Melissa likes her work. I think she likes the travel. But, no, I don't think she liked Chicago much."

"Well, it's one of two things; Melissa's boss Niels is a psychopath, and the best time to leave was yesterday. Or, she could have been a responsible adult and could have planned her departure. She burned bridges with this hasty departure."

Kevin had just pulled his unmarked car into the precinct's parking lot. He turned it off and came around to open my door.

"Melissa Bollinger went 'scorched earth' with her hasty departure. It remains to be seen if it was the smart move."

Kevin walked us through a side entrance, using his keycard to get a heavy door to open.

"Do you think folks do this a lot? That they drop everything and just leave? Start again somewhere knew?"

Kevin scoffed. "All the time. Grown adults have the right to do that. However, it sucks for the people they leave behind. Even more so for us police officers who have to search for the 'missing people,'" he air-quoted, "only to find them living new lives, safely. Then we get to deliver that heartbreaking news to the folks left behind by the runaway adults."

"I don't know why I didn't consider that," I said as we got in an elevator.

"Why would you?" Kevin said as he shrugged. "You're not a cop."

Kevin was right, of course. Still, I tucked away that valuable piece of knowledge. Kevin introduced me to a couple of cops who stopped us. I blushed as he introduced me as his girlfriend. Still, I was polite.

One uniformed police officer had a lot to report to Kevin. I put my hand on Kevin's arm and spoke to him.

"I remember where your desk is. Do you want me to wait for you there?"

"Please, and thank you," he said.

I walked away and headed towards Detective Connelly's desk - my *boyfriend's* desk. His place of work. It made me nervous, I found. Was I supposed to sit on his chair? I couldn't muster the nerve to do so. Instead, I sat on a chair across his desk. I let out a breath and pulled out my phone.

I thought about calling Melissa. I found myself not having the nerve to do that, either. Guilt filled me. My friend had done something rash - something I suggested she do.

"Oh, Marta," I grumbled.

But what was Melissa supposed to do? She was ready to be done with Niels. She said that he was starting to get more controlling and that he was keeping track of what she was doing.

Could Melissa have professionally approached Niels? Probably, but maybe he would have talked her into staying. Maybe Melissa had left because that was the moment for her, inconvenient as it was.

A kiss to the top of my head gave me chills and warmed me up all at the same time.

"What are you ruminating about over there?" Kevin asked as he sat on the chair behind his desk.

"Melissa, and not much else. I'm feeling guilty over the fact that I pushed her to leave."

"She had to go, Marta," Kevin said as he began to rifle through a file on his desk. "Did she have to leave so suddenly? We don't know," he said.

"Have you had dinner?" I asked of him.

Kevin smiled at me. "I have not. Do you want to get take-out for here, or do you want to sit down somewhere?"

I looked around his office and smiled. "I understand if you get tired of this place, but I like it," I said as I turned to him.

Kevin scratched his nose and nodded. "I get it. Take out it is. Pizza?" he asked as he lifted the handset on his desk phone.

"Yeah. New-York Style?"

Kevin set the phone down and stared at me. "Say what?"

"New-York Style. To eat?"

"We haven't had pizza yet, have we?"

I shook my head. "No. Not yet."

"What the hell, Marta? New-York Style?"

"Do you forget that I was raised on the east coast during my first ten years of life?"

"And you've lived here for almost twenty! Long enough for you to correct the error that is your pizza preference."

I scoffed. "Chicago-style pizza is just okay."

Kevin's sharp intake of breath made me laugh. But then the occupant of the desk next to him shook his head.

"I don't know about this one, Kevin," said a dark-haired man I had yet to meet.

"I don't know either, Jeff," Kevin said to the guy.

"Hey!" I said to Kevin.

Kevin shook his head. "We are going to have to shelf this conversation because I have stuff to get to, and also because I am starved."

"Fine," I said as I let out a breath.

"That doesn't sound like the normal 'fine,'" the now-named Jeff said.

"I can handle the heavy lifting from here, Jeff. But thanks," Kevin said.

Staring me down, Kevin picked up his phone and blatantly ordered a deep dish pizza. I laughed, and he smiled.

"You are lucky you are pretty," he said to me as he turned his monitor on.

"You are lucky that you are cute," I said back.

"Stop making me blush. I'm trying to work here," Kevin said as he smiled.

I chuckled and went back to my cell phone. Half an hour later held our pizza dinner consumed.

"Told you deep-dish was good," Kevin said.

"I never said it wasn't!" I protested. "Just that it isn't as good as-"

"Let me stop you right there," Kevin said.

Kevin looked away from me and stared off at a point I couldn't make out. I noticed that Jeff stared, too, as did a couple of other police detectives. I turned back to see what they were looking at.

My jaw dropped as I saw Niels Ericsson standing at the entrance while speaking to a uniformed police detective.

"Oh, my God," I said to Kevin.

"Who is that?" Kevin asked of me.

"That's Niels, Kevin. Niels Erickson."

Chapter Twenty-Four

Kevin's face paled just a touch, but only for a moment.

"Get behind the desk, Marta," he said to me.

"But-"

"Get behind the desk and nd crouch down," he said. "Quick, Marta!"

I did as he requested, even if I didn't understand what was going on. Kevin stood up and removed his jacket. I noticed that he flexed the fingers of his right hand, which was close to his gun.

"Oh, my God," I whispered.

"What the fuck?" Jeff said to Kevin.

"This guy isn't in his right mind, man. Keep your eyes peeled," Kevin said to Jeff.

Instantly, Jeff pushed away from his desk and stood up.

"Ali," Kevin called. "What's going on?"

I assumed that Ali was the police officer who had been speaking to Niels. I heard footsteps approach the desk.

"Hello. My name is Niels Erickson," said Melissa's boss. "I came because my employee sent me an emergency message from here. So here I am."

I covered my mouth with my hand. Niels had just lied - and to at least two police detectives and who knew how many other police officers?

I looked up at Kevin, who looked nonplussed. God bless the man for being a good detective.

"Mr. Erickson?" Kevin calmly said.

"Yes, Erickson."

"My name is Detective Connelly. Who is this person who sent you a message?"

"My employee - Melissa Bollinger. She sent me a message telling me that she was here, but I don't see her."

Niels' convincing lie chilled me so much that I began to shake where I sat. Kevin turned to face Jeff.

"We don't have anyone here named Melissa Bollinger, do we?" he asked Jeff.

"No. No one is actively being questioned," Jeff said.

Kevin turned and faced another side. "Hey, James," he hollered.

James Kostas? I did not know he was there.

"What?" hollered James.

"11-56 question. Do we have a Melissa Bollinger here? Is the name familiar to you?"

Moments later, I heard more footsteps approach Kevin's desk.

"No," I heard James calmly say. "What's this about?"

"I know that Melissa is here," Niels said, and a bit more fiercely. "Please - tell me where she is."

Kevin reached for his jacket, from which he retrieved Melissa's cell phone. He held it up for Niels to view.

"Is this what you were tracking, Mr. Erickson?"

"That is Melissa's phone. Why do you have it?"

Kevin opened the drawer of his desk and placed the phone in it before closing it.

"Did you have Melissa Bollinger's consent to track her cell phone?" Kevin asked.

Niels said nothing.

"Do you know how close you are to the crime that is filing a false police report?"

"I think I will leave now," said Niels.

"I think you are going to stay until I am done talking to you," Kevin said.

Instead of protesting or calling for a lawyer, Niels chuckled.

"Marta?" Niels called out. "Are you here, Marta? I see your cheap leather purse sitting on this detective's chair."

Shit and shit and shit and shit. I stood up, though, as while I was scared, I was not a coward.

"Hello, Niels," I said to him.

Niels looked furious. "Where is Melissa?"

"That's not your concern anymore."

"You nosy little maid!" Niels snapped. "You are sticking your nose where it doesn't belong."

"I am not trying to get on your bad side, Niels, because you are a scary, scary man. But I am still brave enough to tell my friend to get away from you. Melissa's gone and of her own free will."

"You told her to leave me!" Niels yelled.

"Melissa didn't need anyone to tell her to leave you."

Niels took a breath and released it. "You are fired," he said and more calmly.

I nodded. "I understand that. I will have your key cards in the mail tomorrow morning."

"Melissa didn't send you a text, either. You've been tracking her cell phone," I said.

Niels wisely said nothing to that. "I will take my leave now."

"Not so fast," Kevin said. "False police reports and illegal cell phone tracking are against the law."

"I will call my lawyer," Niels said.

Kevin turned to James. "You're up next, I know. I can't take this one."

"I got it," was James' answer.

James turned to me: "Marta? I am going to need you and Kevin to hang out until I am done speaking to Mr. Erickson here."

I nodded. "I'll be here."

"Mr. Erickson. If you could follow me," James politely requested.

Niels let out a breath. "If I could ask Marta one more question."

"No, you cannot," James said, and a bit more firmly. "Please follow me."

Once Niels and James disappeared down a long hallway, I sank on Kevin's desk.

"Can you believe that?" I asked of him.

Kevin went from staring down the long hallway to looking down at me.

"What is it with you and psychopaths?"

I let out a frustrated breath in answer. An hour later held Kevin driving me home. He wasn't saying much.

"That was an interesting conference call," I said to him.

Kevin nodded. "Yes. I was glad to hear Melissa's live voice, as was James. Melissa corroborated her story - your story."

He said nothing after that. His silence concerned me, but not enough to question him about it. I had enough on my mind. When Kevin's car pulled over by my apartment gate, I leaned over and kissed him.

"Marta?"

"Yeah."

"I like your purse. I don't think it looks cheap."

I laughed. "Thank you. And it isn't cheap. It's pigskin, but I like it."

Kevin smiled. "I'm glad."

"Are you okay?" I asked of him.

"Yeah. It was a weird night. I'm still trying to wrap my mind around it."

"You and me both."

"Are you okay?"

I nodded. Kevin reached out and touched my face. "You let me know if Niels bothers you. I want to know just as soon as it happens."

"I will. I think Niels is more a fan of subterfuge, though."

"That doesn't make me feel better."

"I'll let you know if something goes down, okay?"

"Yes."

"Go home," I told him before kissing him again. I then left his car and made my way to my apartment.

Once there, I walked to my kitchen and poured myself a shot of rum, and then another. Melissa was safe. Niels was now a confirmed psychopath. But I was out one friend, and that was sad.

Still, life continued. Heavy in heart, I showed and went to bed.

Chapter Twenty-Five

I woke up with a knot in my throat. I reached for the cell phone on my nightstand and searched for messages.

"*I am home, Amiga. Thank you.*"

My first job of the day was supposed to be Erickson and Associates. Being that I had the time, I lay back down and cried for a little while.

My first stop of the day was the post office. As promised, I shipped my key cards to Ericsson and Associates. Back in my car, I allowed myself to think about Niels' feelings. Was he angry with Melissa and me? Were his feelings hurt? Did he feel betrayed? Did he feel accountable for the mess he'd help make? Was he scared that the cops had gotten the drop on him? Was he plotting his revenge against me?

Maybe Niels was at home, trying to keep his marriage afloat. Perhaps he was at his office, cleaning up the mess left after Melissa's abrupt departure. Maybe Niels was thinking about how he could get back at me.

That was not my problem anymore, though, as I had others. I need to secure a contract with Barney's Haberdashery. If I were lucky, I'd get paid sixty percent of what I'd been clearing with Erickson and Associates, which meant that I would have to find yet another gig.

Pushing those concerns aside, I headed to Jane Knight's place. She was home, which was surprising.

"How goes it?" she asked of me.

I looked at her to try to discern her mood. Jane was dressed and made up. She was reading the paper while drinking some tea. Definitely within normal ranges, then.

"Okay," I said. "And you?"

She nodded. "Getting better, thanks."

"Good."

Jane went back to her paper. I went to the cleaning closet and did my thing. At the pawnshop, Jamie was feeling chatty, which was a welcome distraction.

"Barney's looking forward to your cleaning."

"I am looking forward to his paycheck," was my answer.

Jamie laughed. "Barney's a bit rough around the edges - but don't let that scare you."

Goodness. Not only did I have a smaller paycheck to look forward to, but I also had to worry about a grumpy older man.

"I'll let you know how it goes," I promised.

I cleaned for my two residential customers and then went home. Feeling sad, I called my Mom. I told her everything that had gone down with Erickson and Associates.

"Goodness," she said. "Nothing good ever comes with dating a married man."

"Yes. I would agree with that. Mostly. Anibal's *puta* Gretchen got herself a husband."

Mom scoffed. "That woman got herself the worries of her husband cheating on her. She got herself a roof and a father for her children. Probably not much more than that."

"Not my circus, not my monkeys."

"What does that mean?" Mom asked.

"It just means that Anibal's problems are not my own."

"This is true. But I understand your friend. Sometimes, you have to get away from a bad man. You have to get away and run far. Not always because he's the danger either, but what becomes of you when you are with him."

"That sounds pretty insightful, mom," I said as I sipped coffee.

"It never happened to me, but I know women who shared confidences with me."

I had some more coffee.

"What about your boyfriend? Where is he?"

"Working, I guess. I'm not too sure."

"Don't you care?"

"I'm not his mother, Mom. Also, I am going through my stuff right now. I don't need to hold his hand while I am suffering myself."

"That makes sense, too," Mom said. "But look - you watch out for that rich, crazy man. Men in power don't like hearing the word 'no.' It makes them angry."

"Well, he made an ass out of himself at the precinct, so I think he's going to behave for a while."

At least I hoped so. In any case, I got off the phone with my mother but held it. Kevin hadn't called me in a couple of days. I wondered if the Niels thing scared him off.

"Whatever," I said. I reached for my old standby - the remote control to my DVR.

Chapter Twenty-Six

Two weeks had passed since Melissa had left. My new normal was weird and unwelcome. I missed Melissa something fierce. Jane Knight was working super long hours. My residential customers kept mum, but Jamie was chatty. So was Barney, for that matter.

"I'll tip you if you clean well," said the graying, seventy-eight-year-old man.

"That's fair, Barney."

"Did I tell you that I dressed Perry Como?"

"You did not. I'd love to hear that story."

I swept while I listen to Barney regale me with a story I'd heard twice already. That evening held a date with Kevin.

"How's Barney?" he asked before biting into a chicken wing.

I smiled. "Barney's good. He loves to talk about the old days. He gets a healthy amount of customers, I think, but not while I'm there cleaning."

"That's nice," Kevin said. "A change from Erickson Ventures, huh?"

I let out a breath. "Yeah. The job paid very well. I loved talking to Melissa while I cleaned. And even Niels - when he was keeping his psychopathy to himself - was professional."

Kevin stared at me a bit. "I imagine that Niels' life is a bit tumultuous right now."

I shrugged. "Whatever keeps Niels busy."

"How's Melissa?"

I smiled. "Melissa wrote me a letter. Who does that anymore, right? She's taking it easy - spending time with family and trying to figure things out."

"Do you think she's done with Niels?"

My face fell. "God, I hope so because that's the only smart option. The only healthy one."

Kevin stared at me for a while.

"Can we change the subject?" I asked.

"Of course," he said. "I'm sorry," he said as he covered my hand with his.

I nodded, and he moved his hand. From under my lashes, I watched Kevin. He looked distracted, too.

"Do you want to talk about your cases?"

He looked up at me and shook his head. "I do not."

"Okay," I simply said.

Our occupations made us stick our noses in the lives of others. It wasn't always easy to shake it off, it seemed.

"Wanna watch a movie?" I asked of him.

Kevin's face scrunched up for a second. "Yeah, but I don't feel like driving out to the nice theaters."

"I meant at my place."

His expression instantly changed, and I laughed. "Watching a movie at my place is not a euphemism for sex," I whispered.

Kevin pouted, then shrugged. "Okay. What movie?"

"A Guy Ritchie one I've been wanting-"

"Say no more," he cut off.

We had the waitress bag our food. Thirty minutes later held us in my living room, watching the movie while we ate the food.

"Why isn't 'watching a movie' a euphemism for sex?" Kevin asked.

I paused the movie and turned to him. "What?"

"Sex, Marta. I want to have sex with you."

Kevin's words elicited a tumble of emotions - surprise, delight, fear, lust, and confusion.

"Do you want to have sex with me?"

Crap. I would have to answer Kevin.

"I do," I said as I cleared my throat. "Very much, but...but I'm scared."

"I won't hurt you."

"I've only ever had sex with one man," I blurted.

Kevin's eyes widened. "Really?"

I nodded. "Yeah. I'm careful with it."

"I think that's an understatement."

"Kevin, I like you a lot. So much. But I don't want to rush anything. I don't want to rush myself."

"I would never, ever force anything," he replied, sounding a bit angry.

I let out a breath. "I want to have sex again. I want it to be with you. But I'm not ready. We're still brand-new. Also, the person I have sex with? I want to love him and be loved in return. I want something real."

Kevin reached for his beer and drank from it.

"When's the last time you...had sex?"

"I am not answering that," he said as he set his beer down. "It was before you and I started dating. That's all that matters. Also, I won't cheat on you."

"Good."

"That's not to say that waiting will be easy."

"I know."

He kept staring at me. "But...without getting ahead of things...this," he said as he motioned the air between us, "is real. I want you to know that."

I swallowed at tears. "I think so, too."

"Could you quit talking about sex now? I want to get back to the movie," he teased.

I rolled my eyes and hit play.

A few days later, I met with my financial planner at a new locale

"Krispy Kreme," I said to Ada as I sat across from her. "Cool."

Ada smiled and shrugged. "Why not mix it up?"

"Because you like Panera."

"I am used to Panera. Fast wifi and regular faces. Doesn't mean I shouldn't try something new."

I stared at Ada for a few seconds before looking at the donut-making conveyer belt. "How can employees work here and not get fat?"

"They are all fat," Ada whispered.

"Let me join them then. I'll be right back."

I came back with a couple of glazed donuts and a big cup of coffee.

"I've seen your earnings," Ada said as she glanced at her laptop screen. "You are doing okay. I noticed that you lost that Erickson job, though. What happened there?"

I let out a breath. "I had to move on. I think the business is shuttering and moving back to Denmark, anyway."

Ada nodded. "Okay. You picked up a haberdashery. What is that?"

"Men's clothing store. Tailoring, too. A nice place."

"Have you looked at the HUD home loan links I sent your way?"

I shook my head no and then had a bite of crispy glaze. After chewing it, I spoke. "Not yet. It's daunting. Intimidating."

"Your mortgage might be cheaper than your rent. You need to look into that."

"I'm scared," I confided.

Ada shrugged. "I understand why. Cleaning is not a promise of work, but if you think about it, nothing is promised. Anibal might close shop one day and head back to Puerto Rico."

"Is he?"

She shook her head. "I don't think so, but he could. People lose jobs for all sorts of reasons. But living in fear isn't living. Take a chance."

I was surprised when I felt tears in my eyes. I blinked them away.

"Are you okay?" Ada asked.

I laughed and used the corner of a clean napkin to dry my eye with. "Yeah. Sorry. That's just something a friend of mine would have said. She's recently moved away, though. Starting again, ironically," I said.

"New beginnings are scary but worthwhile. I want you to look at the loan paperwork, okay?"

"Okay. I will."

"But, I did see a purchase that surprised me," Ada said as she glanced at her laptop again.

"What's that?" I asked.

"Cosmetics from Gucci. I get it, they are nice. But a bit pricey. Also, why did you have them delivered to Iowa? Were they a gift?"

"What are you talking about?" I said as I set my donut down.

Ada rifled through a file before showing me something. "Here. It's on the bank statement you forwarded to me."

Shocked, I scanned the statement. There, in a tiny section under my checking account information, was my secured credit card line. It held one charge - to Gucci.

"What in the fuck is this?" I asked.

"This wasn't you?"

"No!" I loudly said.

"Okay. Okay," Ada calmed. "We can report this as a fraudulent charge with your bank. You can get your money back. Also, it's a secured card, right? What's the limit?"

"Fifty dollars," I said. "The credit line is larger, but fifty dollars is the lock."

Having lost my appetite, I stared at my bank statement. "What in the hell?" I said again.

"This happens to most people," Ada said. "Let's call your bank right now."

So, we did. The charge was reversed instantaneously. Out of curiosity, I asked another question.

"Whoever...stole my information...did they try to put more things on my card?"

"Yes - we rejected about three hundred dollars' worth of charges."

"Oh, my God. Is there any way you could send me a list of those charges?"

"Sure thing, Miss Morales. You should have it in your email inbox within the next thirty minutes."

I hung up the phone feeling slightly better. Ada stared at me for a minute and then laughed.

"Why did you ask for those charges?"

"I want to know who's trying to live it up using my credit card."

"Well, I almost feel bad for them," Ada said as she packed up her things. "Of all people, they picked a private investigator to steal money from."

I laughed. It felt good.

I carried on with the rest of my day. When I got home that evening, I was both dreading and looking forward to looking at my email. I printed the list of unauthorized/rejected charges and read them as I walked my living room floor.

The charges were for Gucci, Chanel, Nordstrom, L'Occitane, and Best Buy.

"At least they have good taste," I muttered.

Thinking quickly, I logged onto my bank's website. I scanned my checking and my savings accounts for erroneous charges and did the same for my unsecured credit card. Nothing was out of order.

I'd only ever provided my secured credit card information to one business - Visions of Teeth Dental.

"Edna *fucking* Nazario," I seethed.

Chapter Twenty-Seven

To sleuth or not to sleuth was the question on my mind the following day. I pondered that as I cleaned Jane's condo, Jamie's Pawnshop, Barney's Haberdashery, and one of my two residential customers.

Interestingly enough, my decision to sleuth Edna Nazario came while I vacuumed the bedroom of the college-aged student residing at the home of her parents, which was my second residential gig.

Brendalynn Dean had a colorful array of sneakers. I didn't even recognize the brand name. I finished her room and the others, before bracing myself and going to the living room, where Brendalynn sat with her mother, Carol.

"Yes, Marta? Is everything okay?" Carol asked as she sat her coffee cup down.

"Absolutely, Mrs. Dean. I just finished cleaning Brendalynn's already clean bedroom when I saw her gorgeous shoes."

Brendalynn set her book down and turned to face me. "Wow. I've never heard you say that many words," the redhead said.

"You might never hear me repeat this many again." But I was smiling when I said it.

"You are polite for lying about my daughter's cleanliness," Carol said as she smiled.

I shook my head. "I'm not lying, Mrs. Dean. Typically, kids Brendalynn's age have a lot more biohazards in their room."

That made Brendalynn laugh out loud. "See, Mom? I told you I wasn't that bad."

I shook my head. "I am sorry if I caused your argument."

Brendalynn scoffed. "This is nothing, Marta. You're good."

"Thank you. My question is for you, Brendalynn - if you don't mind answering, that is."

"Shoot," she said as she set her book back down.

"Your shoes. They are just gorgeous - the sneakers you have in different colors?"

"Thank you," Brendalynn said. "I earned every pair, I'll say."

Carol Dean smiled. "I told Brendalynn that she could have five pairs of Woodsy sneakers should she bring home all A's."

"And I did!" Brendalynn said.

"That's great," I said. "Congratulations to you both. I am curious about the shoes because I saw someone with the same kind of shoes - Woodsys - but in peach. Are they expensive, too?"

Brendalynn sat up quickly. "Wait a minute! You saw someone wearing Woodsys in PEACH?"!

145

I nodded. "Yeah. Are the peach ones expensive?"

"Uh, yeah," Brendalynn exhorted. "They go for like seven hundred dollars! And you have to get on a waiting list for them, but only celebrities get the top spots! Woodsys only releases special colored shoes once a quarter - and there are only ten spots. SO, if you saw someone with peach Woodsys - well, chances are they are SUPER loaded."

A picture began to form. Edna Nazario - a dental assistant - was raking in the money. But how? I thanked the Dean family for their help and wished them a good day before going home.

Driving home, I let my mind do some calculations. I'd researched the salary of dental assistants while investigating Edna Nazario for Doña Elena. They did okay financially, making $40k a year on the high end.

Forty-thousand dollars a year wasn't nothing, but it also wasn't much - not in Chicago. Living in a large metropolitan city meant high taxes and high expenses.

Once home, I quickly showered and changed before dashing to my laptop. A general search into 'woodsy shoes' yielded many results. I saw pictures of celebrities wearing them, as well as models wearing them on the runway.

"They're not that cute," I muttered.

But what did a forty-year-old maid know? A search for 'peach woodsy' yielded a handful of images of A-list actresses wearing them, as well as 'influencers.' Blog entries advised how to make it to the waitlist for Woodys seasonal release of highly-coveted shoes, in limited colors.

I closed the lid of my laptop and composed my thoughts. Realizing I needed to be more organized, I reached for a pad and paper. Thinking more about it, I grabbed a manila folder. Using a Sharpie pen, I wrote 'Edna Nazario' on the tab.

"You've caught my notice," I said to the name.

I almost welcomed the unsolicited sleuthing job because of the distraction it afforded. I wasn't seeing Jane much, as she was working late hours at the law firm (perhaps needing a distraction herself). Jamie was friendly, as was Barney. The Deans had become more familiar with me, which was nice. Still, I kept some distance between myself and them as I did not want to get too close. I missed Melissa something fierce. I knew that she was doing alright in P.A., as she'd taken to sending me postcards.

The next day, and after work, I was still curious about Melissa and what might be happening to her. Wanting to pick someone's brain on it, I finished my jobs and went home to call my brother.

"Yo," he said.

I looked at my calendar on my living room wall. "Aren't you working today?"

"I am. What's up?"

"Oh. Wow. I'm just surprised by your polite greeting."

"Don't you think I can be nice? Of course I am nice!" Rafy snapped.

I nodded. "That's more like it. Do you have a minute or two so that I can pick your brain?

"You have seven. If it's interesting, I'll make it ten."

So, I told him everything that went down with Niels and Melissa.

"Okay. You've engaged my interest. I'm upgrading you to fifteen minutes."

I made a mental note to get back at my brother for his condescension.

"My question is this: do you think Niels is still pursuing Melissa? Will he try to stretch his tentacles out to Pennsylvania?"

"That's a good question," Rafy said. "I think that Niels is probably staying close to home and minding his business, as he made an ass out of himself at the precinct. If I were to guess, I'd say that it's probably a plan - getting in contact with Melissa again. If the man is a psychopath, then he wouldn't have liked that she was the one to end things. It hurt his ego and self-esteem. Speaking about ego and self-confidence, you need to watch your back."

I groaned. "Watch out for Niels, huh?"

"Yep. In Niels' mind, he probably thinks that you set him up - making him incriminate himself in front of three police detectives."

"Crap."

"But again, he lost his mind in front of *three* seasoned Chicago Police Department Detectives. Given Chicago's crime rates, those guys are probably the nation's *best* investigators. Niels does not want that kind of attention. If you stay out of his hair, I bet he stays out of your hair. But you HAVE to do that, Marta."

"I am. I intend to. I am not trying to make any more enemies."

"Good."

I then remembered why I called him. "Well, Edna Nazario is back on my radar."

"¡Marayo Parta!" Rafy loudly cussed. "Don't you fucking learn? Why don't you learn? What are you so damned stubborn?! I told you to leave that Doña Elena shit alone, but you don't fucking listen!"

Over the sound of my brother scolding me, I heard footsteps and a door opening and closing. Rafy was outside, I figured. I only interjected once he took a breath.

"Would you like to hear my side of the story?"

"It's the *stupid* side! It's the part of the movie where the audience is asking themselves why the protagonist is being so stupid! They are wondering why she is kicking at a beehive that houses a queen bee with time on her hands, money to spend, and a score to settle! Your audience wants to know why you sent your worker bee - that would be me - into the dangerous hive only to start shit again!"

Rafy took a breath and let it out.

"Well, I'll give you style points," I calmly said to my brother. "That almost sounded rehearsed. Are you taking notes from the movie actors you are providing protection for?"

"Don't you dare be funny," he said, but it sounded like he was smiling.

"Rafy - Edna Nazario stole my credit card information and used it for shopping."

"What? Really?"

"Yes."

I explained that Visions of Teeth Dental Office was the only business I had shared that credit card number with. I also told him about Edna's shady behavior during my appointment at Visions of Teeth. I ended it by telling him about her shoes and their cost.

"Peach Woodsys? Edna Nazario had *peach* Woodsys?" Rafy asked.

"Of all the things I tell you, *that's* what stands out?"

"I am a gentleman of style," Rafy said. "I keep close to the trends."

I shook that off. "So, what do you think?"

"I think you are right. Ain't no way a dental assistant can afford peach Woodsy shoes, unless she has a sugar daddy. But the shoes *and* your stolen credit card? Edna Nazario is getting into some dangerous shit."

"Is it my business?" I asked.

Rafy let out a breath. "I'm going to be honest. It wasn't your business - until she *made* it your business. If I were to guess, the charges she ran up on your card? That wasn't personal. That was a small facet in some bigger operation she's got going on."

"I'm investigating her."

"Normally I'd advise against that. But Edna is doing a fucked-up thing. If she had pulled this thievery on anyone but you, she probably would have carried on with it. The brother in me is at war with the police officer in me. I want you to stay safe, but at the same time, I want you to nail this bitch. It's not like she's stealing from rich people; Edna's taking from everyday folk who want to look nicer. Working-class folks."

"I think so, too. I won't spend much time on this, being that no one is paying me for it."

"Smart thinking. Keep your distance."

"One more question for you: I think she's in cahoots with her co-workers. Do you think they would talk about their thievery at work, or if they might meet somewhere else?"

"Oh, they are meeting somewhere else."

I looked at the clock and cringed. My brother was in the middle of the workday, and I was dragging him into things that had nothing to do with his work.

"Let me let you go. I know you are busy with local stuff."

"Eh. Kind of a slow day over here," Rafy said. I could almost see him shrug as he said it. "But Marta - when you watch, keep your distance."

"I will."

With that, he disconnected.

Rafy's opinions and advice helped me feel more confident about what I was about to do. I smiled as I was excited. It was a good feeling.

Chapter Twenty-Eight

I *really* had to make things up to Kevin. In the past week, I'd rejected two date nights because I was busy scoping out Visions of Teeth. I wanted to go out on dates with Kevin, but I had a bone to pick with Edna Nazario. And Nanette. And whoever else was working the scam.

I'd made a list of employees based on their website. Visions of Teeth had two other locations; one in the suburbs and another in Great Lakes. There was no way I was huffing it up to Great Lakes from Chicago. That could be anywhere over an hour each way.

Still, using the company's website, I compared the employees of those locations to the one at the site of my past evaluation. Some employees worked in two places, but not many.

I was looking at my list - matching employees to cars - while I was parked at the Panera nearby. I would have to move my vehicle within an hour, though, as I'd parked in the same place the night before. I looked at the metered spots alongside the road and saw a couple of empty ones. I was about to climb from the backseat to the front seat when my cell phone buzzed. I was going to ignore it but then saw who was calling me.

"Hey, you," I said to Kevin.

"What are you doing?" he asked of me.

I shrugged. "I'm leaving a job out on the west side. About to get some coffee and head home."

"Can I join you?"

Damn it, damn it, damn it. I couldn't say no to Kevin. If I did, he would think that I was blowing him off or cheating on him. Or even worse, he might find out what I was doing.

"You know what? The coffee out here sucks," I said as I sighed. "How about you get us some awesome cop donuts? I'll make the coffee. I can be at my place in twenty minutes."

"How about you make fried fritters AND some coffee?"

I groaned. "I will counter your offer of donuts, coffee, and fritters to an offer of donuts, coffee, fritters, AND a werewolf movie."

"You spend too much time with lawyers," he said to me.

"Maybe I spend too much time with police detectives," I said - but I was smiling.

Kevin laughed out loud, and I was glad to hear it.

"Touche. I'll be there in twenty-five."

"See you then."

I set my folder aside and climbed into my front seat before heading home.

After a great date night with my boyfriend, I went to bed - alone. The next morning, I got up and rushed through my clients' cleanings before heading to the Visions of Teeth location in Skokie.

The Skokie location was across from a library, which was a Godsend. I paid for parking and planted myself in the backseat while I scoped the front doors of VT.

According to VT's (what I started calling Visions of Teeth) website, Mayra and Nanette worked out of this office as well. I spotted Nanette's Nissan parked in the side parking lot of the dental office.

Two hours into my watch had me questioning my location switch. Why did I come over to Skokie, when I knew that Edna was in the downtown location? The answer was that I wanted to allow some space between my car and the business owners around VT. I'd been parked there for too many nights already. Coming to Skokie allowed for some distance, and maybe some new intel.

Thirty minutes after VT closed, Mayra rushed out of the office. Her curly hair bounced around her head as she dashed from a side door of the building to her car. Her arms were full. She carried a purse, a plant, and a box full of files.

"Whatcha got there, Nanette?" I asked. I took pictures of her, using my digital camera.

Like a gift from Heaven, a breeze blasted the back of my car, went across the street, and hit Nanette, who was jamming things in her back seat. While trying to recover her temporarily lost balance, Nanette dropped the box that held the files.

"You've got to be kidding me," I whispered.

I had to jump into action. Quickly, I climbed into my driver's seat and turned the vehicle on. I drove out of the library parking lot and into the lot across from the dental office. My lights shined on Nanette's face as she scrambled to recover the paperwork she'd dropped. Thankfully, I had the foresight to take pictures of what she was doing.

But pictures were not enough, I knew. I needed to see that paperwork - or at least some of it. Taking a chance, I put my brights on and then opened my window.

"Ma'am, are you alright?" I loudly inquired.

"I'm okay!" Nanette said as she covered her eyes with her free hand.

"You know what? I am going to call the police," I called out.

"No!" Nanette begged. "It's okay."

"There's a fine in Skokie for littering, and you are doing that!" I yelled. "I'm calling the cops!"

Nanette closed her passenger side door and then ran to her driver's side. One minute later had her peeling out of the lot. When I was sure that Nanette was indeed gone, I parked my car and recovered the paperwork she'd lost. Hastily, I grabbed everything and jammed it into a folder. I dashed to my car and drove away.

Chapter Twenty-Nine

I could not believe what I was seeing. So shocked was I that I served myself a slice of cheesecake AND had a short of Bacardi. The creamy sweetness of the cheesecake and the bitter kick of the Bacardi mustered determination in me.

I went back to my dining table and looked at the twenty-three pieces of paper that lay on my dinner table.

The sheets of paper were photocopies of registration forms - dental patient registration questionnaires. The completion dates ranged from two years past to only a few days ago. The forms had names, dates of birth, addresses, places of work, and social security numbers - all the information required for identity theft.

"Jesus Christ. Holy Mother of God," I said.

My hands shaking, I looked at the addresses again. My brow furrowed as I noticed that some of the forms had Iowa addresses while others had Chicago, Illinois addresses.

I paced the floor as I wondered why a dental hygienist would need to take patient registration forms away from an office.

"She's not admin," I muttered.

Maybe the hygienists multi-tasked, but I doubted it. Quickly, I researched the salaries of Dental Hygienists and found that they made twice the amount of money of dental assistants.

"Okay, okay," I said as I paced.

It was identity theft - it had to be. I stopped pacing and stared at the forms. Perhaps Iowa identity theft victims had their information sold or traded for Chicago identity theft victims.

"Why did Nanette have names for both Iowa and Chicago? Do they exchange information at another location?"

It was the only thing that made sense. There was no way they'd use their place of work as a medium to exchange information.

"They make photocopies at the office. They do their scamming elsewhere," I said.

And now I had the names of 23 folks laying on my dinner table. If someone found the forms, I could be accused of identity theft.

"Shit and shit, and shit!" I cussed out loud.

I paced some more. "Think, Marta; think," I said.

I could have gone to Kevin but would have had to tell him what I did to make money on the side. I did not want to do that—also, everything I had violated a chain of custody. I wouldn't call my dad or my brother, as I did not want to get them involved in my mess.

Needing a distraction, I gathered the forms and shoved them into a manila envelope. Out of sight, out of mind. After that, I turned on my TV and DVR. I noticed that I still had an FBI show to watch.

"Of course," I said.

I ran to my computer and found a phone number for the FBI tipline, as well as a mailing address and an email address.

"My prints are all over this stuff," I said as I looked at the manila envelope.

I had to get the information to the FBI without revealing my identity. I knew that images taken from digital cameras left identifiable information behind. That meant that my cell phone and my digital camera were out. Thinking quickly, I grabbed my purse and my keys and ran out to Walmart. From there I purchased a Polaroid-style camera and lots of film. Into my basket went fresh manila envelopes as well.

"There go sixty dollars I won't get back," I said as I scanned the items.

Once home, I used cleaning gloves to assemble the forms on the floor. I took pictures of every single patient registration sheet. After, I placed the developed pictures into a manila envelope. Using my left hand, I carefully addressed the manila envelope to an FBI location in Louisiana. I used tap water to seal it.

I reviewed the postage stamps I had and found them to be a bit too specific.

"Fuck," I said, allowing myself a cuss word.

The post offices were closed for the night; I'd have to wait for the next morning to continue my work. Glad that I had a plan, I went to bed for the night.

The next morning, I called Jane to let her know I'd be late. After that, I packed up my things and headed out.

My first stop was at the parking lot of Dunkin' Donuts, where I sipped a coffee before using a burner and Dunkin Donuts' free wifi in conjunction with my voice recorder.

I then went to a post office where I purchased generic 'Forever' stamps from a machine. If any of the folks within the post office lobby thought it weird that I was using gloves to buy stamps, they said nothing.

I drove to another post office location and parked in their lot. Still wearing my gloves, I over-stamped the envelope while keeping it inside of a clean plastic bag. Once that was done, I drove to a mailbox and dropped it in.

I drove around for another half-hour, trying to find an Office Depot with shredding services. Once there, I walked in, carrying a big box of things I'd printed the night before.

Faking an accent in English, I spoke to an employee. "Hello. I am here for my boss," I said to a bored-looking cashier. "I came to shred things?"

"Uh...yes. What kind of paperwork?" asked the clerk.

That was none of his business. "Accounting paperwork. Lots of numbers, I no understand," I said as I smiled.

"Fine. We'll weigh your paperwork and get you started."

"Thank you!"

I'd hidden the confidential paperwork within the hundred bogus balance sheets I'd printed. The clerk weighed my forms and then wrote a receipt for me.

"You take cash?"

"Yes," he said. "You can go ahead and shred them here. Bring the shredder receipt when you finish."

"Thank you!"

As soon as he left my side, I fed the forms into the triple-A certified safe shredder, whatever that meant. Once I that was complete, I grabbed the receipt and my box before heading to the cashier, where I paid in cash.

"Would you like to sign up for an Office Depot credit card?"

I laughed. "Oh, no. I do so bad with credit. Make my husband *angry!*"

The clerk nodded, looking disinterested. He handed me my change and wished me a good day.

If only.

I drove for a while, trying to find a payphone that wasn't close to anything resembling a video camera. Having found one by a park, I pulled over and walked to it. Using my gloves, I took a breath and dialed the 1-800 number. After hitting a couple of buttons, a live person came on the phone.

"Good morning, this is-"

I had no time for niceties. I hit the play button on my portable voice recorder and listened as my distorted voice gave information.

"*Visions of Teeth Dental with offices on 14505 North Milwaukee Avenue in Chicago as well as the office on 1621 Hollingwood Avenue in Skokie are participating in an identity theft ring. They are exchanging information gleaned off of dental registration forms and are trading them with a dental office in Iowa. Participants in this scheme are Nanette Kreef and Edna Nazario. Their current victims are as follows: Jane Marcel, Marie Lerz, Javier Dominguez, Joseph Zielinski, Lana Boxer, Maria Vega, Mark Matthews, Wyatt Storm, Maria Kuzca, Victoria Washington...*"

"Who is this?" asked the person handling the FBI tip line phone call.

The call was being recorded, I knew, so I ignored the question and let my recording continue.

"*Retrieved patient registration forms for the identity theft victims have been mailed to your address in Baton Rouge, Louisiana. Nanette Kreef - an employee of Visions of Teeth feels remorse for her actions and will be more likely to confess than Edna Nazario.*"

That was it - all I had to say. I hung up the payphone and walked away. I thanked God for the chilly late January blast, as it gave me a reason to wear a black scarf and a black knit cap. While I knew that the FBI could trace my call as soon as it was placed, I still hurried as I didn't want a passerby to be able to identify me later.

As soon as I got into my car, I turned it on and drove away. Once I was about a half a block away from the phone, I removed my scarf and my hat.

"Got you back, Edna," I said to no one in particular.

Chapter Thirty

Of all days to be home, Jane Knight, esquire, chose that late morning to be in residence.

"Long time no see," she said to me.

I stared at her for a bit. She was at her breakfast table, drinking coffee while she read her paper.

"Likewise," I said before walking to the coat closet to hang up my jacket and gloves.

"You are looking rough for wear," Jane commented.

I let out a breath and stared at her. "Rude."

She chuckled. "You are not looking unattractive. You simply look unrested."

"It's because I am unrested. But, still perfectly functional."

Wanting to shake her off, I decided to start cleaning upstairs. Undeterred, the lawyer followed me. I ignored her as I retrieved the cleaning products from the upstairs closet and began to clean.

"What have you been up to?" Jane asked as she leaned on her bathroom door.

Damn and damn. I couldn't maintain my silence, as much as I wanted to. Jane Knight was my client but was also my sometimes-attorney. Also, she was friendly, and she didn't have many of those. Neither did I, for that matter.

"Why do you think criminals get sloppy?" I asked as I sprayed her shower walls using a non-toxic green cleaner.

Jane laughed out loud. "Never a dull moment with you."

I smiled but continued cleaning.

"For the most part, criminals get sloppy because they get lazy. They get away with enough things that they feel invincible."

I nodded. "I can see that."

"Marta?"

"Yeah."

"Do you have a dollar?"

I set my sponge down and turned to her. "Sure. Why?"

"Give me a dollar," she said.

I went all the way downstairs to my purse, where I retrieved a dollar. I came upstairs and handed it to Jane.

"There," Jane said as she took the dollar from me. "What's on your mind?"

I went back to scrubbing her shower walls for a moment. "Someone stole money from me. I got it back and then some."

"That doesn't sound ominous," Jane said as she sat on the toilet.

I let out a breath. "I didn't harm anyone, but it's a long story. Do you have an hour or two?"

"I do."

So, I told her everything about Edna Nazario. Heck, I even told her about Doña Elena. After that, I told her Melissa and Niels.

By the time I was done with my tales, I'd finished her upstairs bathroom and the rest of the upper level. I'd even completed the office and was now working on her fridge.

"Goodness gracious. No one's life is as exciting as yours."

I groaned. "Exhausting is what it is." I let out a yawn while I was at it. "But...I can corroborate what you know. Criminals get sloppy because is it a pain in the rear to commit a clean crime."

"Well, you did a good job of covering up your tracks."

"Thank you," I said to her.

Done with the fridge, I moved onto the countertops. "How are you?" I asked of her.

She shrugged. "Staying busy at work."

"Did Tim tell you that he tried to poach me?"

Jane's green eyes widened. "He did WHAT?!"

I laughed. "I told Tim that I am staying right here."

"That fucker," Jane said but sounded less angry.

I shrugged. "Are you going to be okay to get your dinner?"

Jane shook her head. "No need. I'll be getting dinner at work tonight."

"Cool."

Jane stared at me a bit. "You advised Melissa well."

I was stunned into silence, but only for a few moments. "You think so?"

"Yes. When dealing with a dangerous, powerful man? You find an emergency exit and barrel towards it."

"Yeah," I said as I swallowed at tears.

Jane laughed. "And if a bad guy crosses Marta Morales? Well, it's game over for him or her, isn't it?"

I smiled and shook my head. "I'm just trying to make a living."

"Aren't we all?"

Chapter Thirty-One

I took it easy over the next few days. All I did was clean. I had nothing to do with investigative work, as I was exhausted. Except for telling Rafy that the "situation had been handled," I didn't even think about it. Investigating Edna and her cohorts, and then reporting them to the correct authorities without incriminating myself had left me exhausted.

So, I cleaned, I watched TV, and I stuffed my face. One week after having called the FBI, I had Kevin over for dessert.

He looked exhausted himself. I brought him a slice of cheesecake to the couch while he vegged out to a TV show on aliens.

"What's taking it out of you?" I asked of him.

Kevin shook his head. "Murder. Fucking murder." He let out a breath. "People are so horrible to each other."

"Eat," I said. "It helps."

Kevin smiled. "Okay."

He moaned in pleasure as he had a bite of the cheesecake. I was happy to bring even a bit of goodness his way. After having his slice, he looked at me.

"How do you look so hot wearing sweatpants and a t-shirt?"

I laughed. "You must be looking at some ugly guys all day, I guess."

He let out a breath and rested his head on the back of my couch. I reached over and gently pushed back the red curls that had landed on his forehead.

"That feels good," he whispered.

"I love your hair."

"Wanna fuck?"

I groaned and pulled my hand back. Kevin laughed and grabbed it. "I'm just teasing, Marta. I know you aren't ready."

"Then why do you say stuff like that?"

He shrugged. "To break the tension, I guess."

"Intimacy is about far more than sex," I said to him.

"I know that. Sitting here with you is intimate. I like it. A lot."

I smiled again. I smiled even further when Kevin took the dessert plates back to the kitchen. I lay back on the couch and closed my eyes for a moment.

"Marta?"

"Yeah," I said, not opening my eyes.

"Who's Edna Nazario?"

Chapter Thirty-Two

Alarmed, my eyes shot open. Kevin was NOT supposed to know about Edna Nazario. Shit and shit. How was I supposed to act? How was I supposed to react?

How did I keep that big a secret from my police detective boyfriend? Instantly, I knew what I had to do.

I groaned and stood up. I then made my way to the dining room table, where a manila folder sat under a magazine. 'Edna Nazario' was written on the tab of the folder.

What had I been *thinking*? Why didn't I get rid of that??!!

"Are you going through my things, detective?" I calmly asked.

"No. I looked at the magazine on there when I saw it."

"Oh? The Real Simple magazine? On cleaning and home decorating?"

"Fine, Marta. I snooped."

"Not cool, Kevin."

"Why do you have a file on a person named Edna Nazario?"

I let out a breath. "Because Edna Nazario stole my money."

Kevin turned to face me. "Excuse me?"

"Let's go to the kitchen. I'll make you some coffee while I tell you about it."

Giving him my back while I made the coffee helped calm me. I told Kevin that I went to a dental office to look into getting my teeth whitened. I added that I'd only shared my credit card information with them and no one else, which was why I suspected them.

"Why did you focus on her - Edna Nazario?"

"Edna Nazario gave me a bad vibe. She was unhappy that I wouldn't share my social security number with her. She gave me an attitude and kicked me out."

"Why didn't you tell me this? I am a cop, you know," Kevin angrily said.

"Because...a bad feeling isn't proof. Also, while I am sure that it was the dental office that misappropriated my credit card information, it wasn't evidence. And I got my money back from my credit card company. The situation is handled now. I just hadn't gotten rid of the file."

"If you had a file folder, it meant you had papers. Where are the papers?"

"Wait a minute. Did you look in the file?!"

Kevin, presumably ashamed, looked away from me.

"What gives you the right, Kevin?!"

He said nothing for a bit. "You don't tell me everything, Marta."

"You're right! I don't!"

"I feel like...there's stuff you don't tell me. Like you are hiding things."

"Because I am! We JUST started dating! You are my first boyfriend in a long time, so yes, I am not telling you everything. But I also don't push you to tell me everything," I argued.

"What aren't you telling me?"

"You aren't entitled to that information!"

"I don't want to fight," he said as he slowly stood up.

"Too late, Kevin! You went through my things and demanded answers."

"I'm sorry, okay? I can't turn the nosy thing off."

"It's fine to be nosy. I understand that. But it doesn't mean that you are entitled to answers."

Kevin let out a breath. "I'm sorry, Marta."

"Me too. I think you should go."

Kevin's face fell. "I'm sorry."

"I know. But I'm tired. Maybe you are, too. I think we should call it a night."

I walked to the door and opened it. Kevin grabbed his things and met me at the door.

"Do you still like me?" he asked.

I rolled my eyes. "Yes, but you make me mad."

"I'm sorry," he said as he touched my face.

"I know. I'm not mad. I just want to call it a night."

"Okay. Lock up, okay?"

"Yeah. Drive safe."

He gave me a peck and then left. When I heard his steps descend, I let out a breath.

"Fuck you, Edna Nazario," I said as I snatched the file folder and tore it into pieces.

Chapter Thirty-Three

Edna fucking Nazario was the gift that kept giving. One week later, I was at home watching evening TV when Kevin called me.

"Hey, you," I said to him.

"Do you have your phone handy?"

"I'm talking to you on it."

"I'm texting you a news link."

"Of what?"

"Watch it and call me back."

Kevin hung up. Nervously, I checked my messages and found the link. It went to a news report on the FBI raiding Visions of Teeth Dental Office.

My hands shook as I watched a scrubs-clad Edna being taken into custody by a man wearing an FBI-emblazoned jacket. Also arrested were Mayra and Nanette. Instantly, I called Kevin.

"Wow," I simply said.

"You could have taken the words right out of my mouth, Marta," he angrily said.

"Why are you mad?"

"Why don't you sound more surprised?"

"I am surprised. Also, you keep cutting me off! Why are you taking issue with me?"

"Because you are fucking lying, Marta! I caught you in a lie, and I am pissed off. You knew this would go down!" he yelled.

An odd combination of fear and anger took residence within me.

"Who am I talking to? Huh? The boyfriend or the police detective?"

"I am one and the same."

"I don't like either one of you right now. Not at all. You need to leave me alone for a while, Kevin."

"I am not doing that!" he snapped. "I'm outside your gate right now. Open up."

I hung up and began to shake. Still, I put my coat on and walked down the stairs and outside. Kevin stood outside the gates.

"Let me in," he said.

"I don't like your tone, but I don't fancy arguing outside, either."

Two minutes later held Kevin inside of my apartment.

"Marta. What did you do?" he asked of me.

"I investigated Edna Nazario."

"Who gave you the right to do that?!" he barked.

"Which amendment are you referring to?"

"What?" he asked, his face screwed up.

"Would that be Amendment 4? The one *you* violated?"

Kevin took a breath and released it. "You just confirmed what I already knew," he said as he pointed to me. "You called the FBI."

I crossed my arms over my chest but said nothing.

"You are so fucking smart, Marta."

"Why is that a problem?" I asked of him.

"It isn't! But it's a problem for me when you use your smarts to play around with laws and expect me to look the other way!"

"What laws have I broken?!"

"You snooped, Marta! I don't know how you did it, but you did. You got information to the FBI without leaving a trace of evidence, which is fucking scary. For me."

I took a breath and looked out the window. It was snowing. When did that start?

"Are you going to answer me?" Kevin asked.

I was going to say something smart but changed my mind.

"Why are you hounding me about this, Kevin?"

Some of the wind left his sails. "Because you doing things like this? I think this was what I was sensing before - that you were snooping and not telling me about it."

"I don't want to fight with you, Kevin."

"Then tell me what you did."

Tears filled my voice. "You aren't entitled to that. Not as a detective, and not as my boyfriend."

"I don't see how we can make this work, Marta," Kevin said. His voice was shaking.

I started crying. "I'm in love with you. There's so much to be in love with," I said as I tried to sniff tears away. "But...the last time I gave my truths and my desires away, I lost so much. It took so many tears and so many years to get it back."

Kevin wiped his eyes and let out a breath. "So, that's it? You won't tell me what you did?"

Admitting doing something - anything - was admitting too much.

"Why do you get to be the only one who is entitled to keep secrets?"

"Because that's my job. It isn't personal. But your keeping shit from me is personal."

I stood right there - at the precipice - wondering what to say and what not to say.

"I need time," I said to him.

Kevin nodded. "I'll give it to you, Marta, because I need time, too. We can pick this thing up just as soon as you tell me what you did."

He didn't even kiss me goodbye. He just left.

Chapter Thirty-Four

The damned detective kept his word. Two weeks had passed since Kevin and I had gone on a break.

I missed him so much. But I couldn't call him. If I did, he would demand answers that I could not trust him with. But if he called me, it meant that he accepted that he'd gone too far.

So, I was without a boyfriend. Again. And that hurt so much because I was in love. Jane commented on my depressed condition, and I told her about it.

"You intimidate him, you know," Jane said.

"How so?"

"Detective Connelly is pretty sure that it was you who called the FBI. But how? There were no fingerprints on the images or the envelope, and your voice was anonymized when you called the FBI's office. The FBI cannot connect the call to you, and neither can Kevin. Also, you got your hands on confidential information in some way he cannot determine. You are his match, if not more so. He is an alpha male, and let me tell you; alpha males do *not* like alpha females."

I burst into tears. Carefully, Jane helped me to a chair at her table.

"I like him. So much," I said as I tried to pull back the tears.

"I am sure Kevin's in love with you, too," she kindly said. "But he might want you to be the sweet, smart, pretty, blue-collar, available girlfriend that he thought you were. He liked that package. But he's realized that he put you in the wrong box, and that *scares* him."

"Am I scary? I don't want to be scary."

Jane's eyes filled with tears. "I don't either," she said, her voice as firm as ever. "But it's who we are. Don't dim your light for a man who wants to shine brighter than you."

I sobbed into my hand for a few seconds.

"Stop crying," Jane said.

For some reason, I did.

"How are you consoling me?" I asked of her. "I thought I'd been consoling you."

Jane beamed. "You have been - even when you are not here. Now I can console you."

I would have hugged her, but I didn't as I didn't want to push things. Instead, I put her crock-pot dinner together and thanked her again. It was enough.

Feeling sad but oddly buoyed at the same time, I carried on with my jobs. I cleaned for Jamie, Barney, the Dean family, and the other residential family whose names I tried to ignore.

My apartment felt like a tomb. I cried as I let myself in.

I wanted to call Kevin, but I knew that I couldn't. I realized that while I could give him my heart, and eventually, my body, I could not give him my identity.

My unlicensed private investigator couldn't hug me or hold me or ask me about my day, though.

I showered and had a light dinner and carried on with the rest of the motions of my evening. On a whim, I checked my mail. What I found there made me start crying again. I tore open the envelope and began to read.

"Hello, Marta. It's me - Waleska. I am so sorry that it's taken me so long to get back to you."

My tears dotted the page. Still, I continued to read.

"Grief is a wild animal, I think - a beast of changing forms. One day, you think you know it and recognize it. But then it shifts shape and jumps from a corner, taking you by surprise all over again."

"I know that no one knows grief as I do - maybe you feel it even more so than I. But I think that I might have that unwelcome edge, as I mourn for my son's father. That's my weight to carry that one day I will shift to him."

I'd forgotten how wonderful a writer Waleska was. Suddenly, I remembered Hector calling me from his base to tell me about the beautiful, heartbreaking letters Waleska mailed him.

"But I am ready to see you again, Marta. And don't mind my parents! They've gotten so used to being my everything that they've forgotten that there are more people out there. So, please call me. Adan and I cannot wait to see you again."

I wanted to call her, but I was too busy sobbing. Ten minutes later, I composed myself enough to call her.

"Hello, Waleska? It's me, Marta."

I heard laughter from her side of the line. "Marta! Hello! It's so good to hear from you."

Not as good as it was to hear from her.

###

En Mi Viejo San Juan/In My Old San Juan

In 1942, a composer named Noel Estrada wrote a song called "En Mi Viejo San Juan." It's a beautiful song known all around the world. It is especially heart-rending for Puerto Ricans living on the mainland who miss the island of Puerto Rico. For your understanding, I've translated the lyrics from Spanish to English. I cannot get through this song without crying. If you read the words, maybe you'll understand why.

En mi viejo San Juan
Cuántos sueños forjé
En mis noches de infancia
Mi primera ilusión
Y mis cuitas de amor
Son recuerdos del alma

In my old San Juan
How many dreams did I forge?
In my nights of infancy
My first hope
And my anxieties of love
Are memories of my soul.

Una tarde me fui
Hacia extraña nación
Pues lo quizo el destino
Pero mi corazón
Se quedó frente al mar
En mi Viejo San Juan

One afternoon I departed
To that strange nation
Because that's what Destiny wanted
But my heart
Stayed in front of the sea
In my old San Juan

Adiós (adiós adiós)
Borinquen querida (tierra de mi amor)

Adios (adios adios)
Mi diosa del mar (mi reina del palmar)
Me voy (ya me voy)
Pero un dia volveré
A buscar mi querer
A soñar otra vez
En mi viejo San Juan

Goodbye (goodbye, goodbye)
Borinquen dearest (land of my love)
Goodbye (goodbye, goodbye)
My goddess of the sea (my queen of the palm grove)
I'm leaving (I'm leaving now)
But one day I will return
To find my love
To dream again
In my Old San Juan

Pero el Tiempo pasó
y el destino burló
Mi terrible nostalgia
y no pude volver
Al San Juan que yo amé
Pedacito de patria

But time passed
And Destiny mocked
My terrible nostalgia
And I could not return
To the San Juan that I loved
Little piece of my homeland

Mi cabello blanqueó
y mi vida se va
Ya la muerte me llama
y no quiero morir
Alejado de ti
Puerto Rico del alma

My hair went White

And my life leaves me
And death calls me now
And I don't want to die
Far away from you
Puerto Rico of my soul

Adiós (adiós adiós)
Borinquen querida (tierra de mi amor)
Adiós (adiós adiós)
Mi diosa del mar (mi reina del palmar)
Me voy (ya me voy)
Pero un dia volveré
A buscar mi querer
A soñar otra vez
En mi viejo San Juan

Goodbye (goodbye, goodbye)
Borinquen dearest (land of my love)
Goodbye (goodbye, goodbye)
My goddess of the sea (my queen of the palm grove)
I'm leaving (I'm leaving now)
But one day I'll return
To find my love
To dream again
In my old San Juan

—Noel Estrada
(translated by Cyndia Rios-Myers)

Hello, Reader!

Did you enjoy reading *Marta Bleaches Everything* as much as I enjoyed writing it? I do hope so.

If you did, would you please do me a solid and leave me a review? I'd love it if you shared your opinion with others, even if you were just okay with it. But especially so if you enjoyed it.

Thank you in advance for going to Amazon and leaving a review.

About the Author

Cyndia Rios-Myers is a Pittsburgh, Pennsylvania-based writer and essayist who enjoys reading, running, good laughs, and nice naps. You can keep up with her musings on her Facebook page, on Instagram @milipan, on her website at www.cyndiariosmyers.com, or Twitter at @criosmyers.

Other Titles by Cyndia Rios-Myers:

Women's Fiction/Detective Titles:

Marta Cleans Up: Book One of the Housekeeping Detective Series

Nice Shootin', Tex!

Joppa Park

Horror/Fantasy Titles:

Rescued by the Wolf: Book One of the Wolves

Gifted by the Wolf: Book Two of the Wolves

Mated by the Wolf: Book Three of the Wolves

Condemned by the Wolf: Book Four of the Wolves

Defended by the Wolf: Book Five of the Wolves

Unveiled by the Wolf: Book Six of the Wolves

Razed by the Wolf: Book Seven of the Wolves

Made in the USA
Monee, IL
07 April 2022